The Path to Horn Cottage

A Cunning Folk Mystery

Prudence S Thomas

Dedication

In memory of a great friend who encouraged me to read
Terry Pratchett when we were children.

A good book recommendation is one of the best gifts a
friend can give, in my opinion.

Acknowledgments

With many thanks to my editor, Susan Cunningham and cover designer, Rena at Cover Quill … and my mother and partner for their love, encouragement and patience.

Author's Note

The Cunning Folk Mysteries are set in a fantasy version of Lancashire, with a different history to our own. I wanted to be able to explore what life would have been like for men and women who could be described as magical practitioners in an alternate history where Christianity had not spread widely after the fall of the Roman Empire. In my imagined old England (which I have named Albion), there is a strong emphasis on trade and scholarly excellence, rather than on colonialism. Meanwhile the rest of Europe has begun to reach out into the world under the banners of Christian missionaries, placing Albion in a precarious position.

I have taken some liberties with Lancastrian place names for my invented world. Apologies to any Lancastrians or lovers of Lancashire who notice this – consider it a homage to your lovely land's fascinating landscape and history.

Prudence S Thomas

Chapter 1

Meryall put her weight against the hard brush and scrubbed the last of the winter ashes from the hearth. Though the mornings were still raw, the days were beginning to lengthen, and it was time to clear away the dust and dirt of winter, to welcome in the fresh new light and air of spring. Tonight, there would be a full moon – the seed moon, when the ground was fertile, growing warm and welcoming to the grains and seeds scattered there.

She dusted the many bottles and jars on her shelves, with jars of demon chaser salve and sage oil, a pot of blackthorn spikes and many powdered herbs, spices and resins, ready to be dispensed into twists of paper or containers her customers brought with them.

It was gloomy inside the ancient cave house. The sun had not gained enough strength to penetrate the little diamond-paned windows, and the light came chiefly from the fire in the broad recessed stone hearth. The ingeniously built rooms were shaped around the natural recesses of the stone, carved by the flow of ancient waters. Meryall did not know how long ago the hands of her ancestors had taken tools and carved out windows and shaped the walls and ceilings to the smooth, curved lines of Horn Cottage. Here and there were marks that she could not quite make out – perhaps runes or carved lines to represent animals or people.

Although the weakness of the spring sunshine made the cave house dull, the walls were freshly whitewashed, and the thick wood of the mantelpiece and the sturdy furniture had been polished to a deep shine, holding the gentle scent of beeswax in their grain.

Throwing the ashes out of the door into the garden, Meryall set water to boil for a tisane and sat with her almanack in her lap, reading by the light of the fire. The morning had been filled with activity. In between her brewing and charm making, three customers had visited her. The first, a plain-faced young man who blushed so much that it seemed that he would scarce be able to tell Meryall what he needed, eventually owned that he was having difficulties in performing the act of love with his sweetheart. Meryall was curious as to why he had visited her rather than Madoc – this was an area where their range of services intersected. The young man had blushed still deeper and said that he had spoken to Madoc already and that his opinion was that this was a matter of the heart or spirit rather than a malady of the body. Meryall took select herbs from her shelves and ground them with salt. This mixture she poured into a tiny scrap of cloth, bound it with red thread and whispered words into the little packet. Meryall took out a piece of cloth to make up a package for the lad, adding a bundle of herbs to prevent conception, explaining how his lady should use them, if they wished to wait a little longer before bringing children into the world. She instructed the young man to place the charm under his pillow and to give offerings to the gods at the next full moon of fresh spring flowers and sent him on his way, still with reddened cheeks, but stuttering his thanks and smiling. The two customers who followed were sisters – women in their middle years who sought divination to help them decide on the most auspicious day to reopen the village inn, under their management.

They chatted pleasantly for some time with Meryall, while she prepared divination materials and departed satisfied, with promises that Meryall should be given a good meal on her first visit.

Meryall glanced up at the sun as she showed the sisters out – it was noon, and she was hungry and in need of a drink – her throat was parched from much talking. She ate two soft oatcakes left over from breakfast, spread with bramble jam, and put water to boil for a tisane. The kettle had begun to sing when she heard a soft tap at the door. Rising from her old wheelback chair, she crossed the kitchen and opened the heavy oak door wide. Her eyes met those of a stranger – a young man of not more than twenty, with neat, handsome features and dark eyes.

'Welcome, do you wish to buy herbs, or to sit for divination?' The young man looked surprised. Meryall smiled.

Most people expected a cunning woman to be old – a

wise crone with silvered hair and gnarled hands. Meryall was well proportioned and attractive, not far off her third decade and with a glossy head of dark hair and green eyes set in a handsome, regular-featured face. She had been the cunning woman of the village of Thornton Cleveleys since the sudden death of her mother when she was just eighteen years of age.

Meryall gestured him into the cottage, pulling a kitchen chair over so that the young man could sit opposite her at the hearth. He took the seat, smiling in thanks.

'Thank you, Mistress Meryall.' His voice was rather higher than she had expected – he cleared his throat, looking embarrassed and resumed in a deeper tone. 'I was hoping that your skill in divination could help me to find someone.'

Meryall looked at him for a long moment. 'It depends on the purpose for which you mean to find them. I will not seek someone who does not wish to be sought or who you mean any harm to–'

'Oh no! I am seeking my sister, mistress. I am Avery Greenhalgh – my younger sister, Eda, has disappeared from the place where she was living and working, Lune Castle. She is just nineteen years of age. I fear that something may have happened to her.'

'You are sure that she has not found a lover and taken off to find an adventure?' Meryall still looked serious and unconvinced. Avery sighed deeply, putting his head in his hands.

'I had word from one of the maids she served with that Eda had gone missing three days ago. I rode immediately to the castle only to be told that she was gone. I demanded to search her quarters at the castle. There was no sign of her, but I noticed a scrape on the stone floor to the side of what I was told was her bed, as if something heavy had been dragged there. The lord of the castle would allow me to search no longer and simply said that she had left his service and had made no mention of any message for me, but I know this cannot be true. It would be most unlike my sister to do so.'

'I do not recognise you – you are not from Thornton Cleveleys. Are your parents still living?' Meryall asked.

'No, we come from Fleetwood. We lost both of our parents to a plague that swept our village some years ago. Eda and I lived alone until she came of age and entered service at the castle.'

Meryall looked at him thoughtfully. 'Fleetwood has a cunning woman of its own – Mistress Melia Mott. Why are you not seeking her help?'

'I did! Mistress Melia said that in a matter of such seriousness, your divination skills were strong, although…' Avery blushed.

Meryall smiled – she knew that her divination skills were well developed. She knew too that she had much to learn in other areas of the cunning arts and that her fellow cunning folk were mindful of the early age at which she had taken up the role of cunning woman and the loss of learning that the loss of her mother had comprehended.

Meryall stood, placing her hand on Avery's shoulder.

'I will try my best to help you. Let me make us some

tisane; you must be tired and overtaxed.' She moved about her cupboards and shelves, taking out two of the mugs she had shaped and baked with a salt glaze the previous midsummer, with their ram's head handle ornament, her pot and pinches of herbs. The scent of lime blossom, catswort and mayweed rose as she poured water onto finely ground herbs. Meryall set the tisane aside to brew, with a jar of honey and a spoon laid out at a small table by Avery's elbow.

She opened a drawer in the dresser and took out a scrap of parchment, a quill and a pot of oak gall ink.

'What is your sister's full name?' She scratched the name Avery gave in dark ink, adding a complex symbol with a flourish of her quill. Meryall took a bundle of dragon's claw, bound the parchment around the dry leaves tightly with thread and tossed it into the fire, taking her seat and turning to face the flames.

'Pour tisane for us both in five minutes, but otherwise be still and do not talk to me.'

Meryall let her eyes rest deep within the fire, looking beyond the flames and feeling a stillness fill her like a mist rising about her. She sensed herself grow tall and wide, extending beyond her physical form. Meryall gazed down through a thick forest into a clearing edged by a stream. A wolf howled somewhere in the woods, and she saw the faint flicker of a fire. Drawing nearer, she saw a small camp, three men seated around the fire and – bundled under a large grey mantle, a figure, awkwardly positioned. She caught a glimpse of a delicate female face within the folds of the cloak, dark hair falling out of her braid and eyes focused on the fire.

As the girl shifted her gaze towards one of the men, Meryall saw a small mark on her brow, an old scar, perhaps. The nearest man stood, taking a drinking vessel to her and holding it to her. As the girl drank, Meryall noted the man's sword belt, reddish hair, heavily muscled body and good, sturdy leather boots. The smoke of the fire hid the other two men from view. Her vision began to pull away. In the fading images, Meryall saw horses tethered amongst the trees and noted an unusually large grey mount.

Sitting back, Meryall reached across to take the tisane Avery had poured into her cup.

'Does your sister carry a mark upon her brow?'

Avery nodded. 'Yes, from a fall when she was a small child. Did you see her?' He leaned forward, his cup held tightly in his hands.

Meryall looked away from him. 'Yes, I believe so. I saw her with three men in a clearing in the woods. I cannot tell if she was there willingly, although she appeared unharmed.'

Avery rubbed his hands over his face, sitting silent and pale for some time.

'She would not leave the castle without telling me; I cannot believe that she has gone willingly.'

'Do you have kinsfolk to help you take your case to the sheriff?' Meryall said, in an effort to bring the young man back to himself.

'No. I am unsure if it would be wise to take this matter to the sheriff, in any case, mistress. I believe the lord of the castle may be involved and if that is so, the sheriff of this place is unlikely to be willing to investigate or intervene.

Lord De Lune stands as sheriff of his town.'

'Well, if you are skilled in tracking, I have an idea where the clearing I saw could be.' Meryall drew a rough map with her quill, handing it to Avery with a gentle smile. 'I hope you find her, friend, but I would urge you to seek the help of the sheriff or at the very least take a companion. It may be dangerous for you to seek her alone.'

Avery took the map, placing it in the pouch at his waist.

'Thank you, mistress.' He turned to go. Meryall watched him as he closed the gate and walked through the woods.

Meryall's cottage was rarely quiet for long on the days when she welcomed visits. A number of customers graced her hearth as the afternoon stretched on. A young woman seeking divination to know whether or not a handsome blue-eyed fisherman was her true love, a man seeking a charm to dispel bad dreams and a new mother seeking a protection charm for her baby – and some herbs to ensure that she did not have any more children just yet. Meryall dealt with them all with grace and common sense, but a lingering disquiet drew her mind back to Avery Greenhalgh and his sister.

She sat down by the fire with a bowl of broth as the sun set. She was in an uncommonly dark mood. Usually Meryall enjoyed her life as the cunning woman of Thornton Cleveleys. The ways of the cunning folk were in her blood – the gifts were inherited, although they needed to be refined through apprenticeship. Her mother and grandmother before her had served the people of their village and the walls of the cave house hummed with the memories of her cunning folk ancestors. However, today she was weighed down by the burden of the vocation, tired by the concerns of her visitors and distracted by her worry about Avery.

Guiltily, she pushed away thoughts about wishing another life for herself – though she loved him dearly, she was envious of Madoc's adventures overseas. The freedom to leave the village and seek adventure, wealth and knowledge had always danced beyond her horizons. Each village had a cunning man or woman. Often, the cunning folk had belonged to the same family and served that village for generations, as in her case. She could not just leave the village without a cunning woman; it was her duty to serve. Meryall sighed. When Madoc had set out on his journeying overseas, he had invited her to go with him. Excited and much in love, she had immediately agreed, but the death of her mother in the few weeks they had taken to prepare for their journey had knocked her off course.

The loss had been a heavy blow, and Meryall grieved sorely even now for her mother, but she had also mourned the loss of that taste of freedom she had missed. Madoc had stayed in the village, promising not to leave without her, for some time. Meryall had watched his patient, kind face over the long summer after her mother's death and knew that he did not resent giving up his adventure. But she found that she resented him giving up his adventure and could not bear to be the reason for it. She had pushed him to leave. He had come back to her after two years, tanned, happy and full of stories of his experiences in faraway lands. She loved to hear him talk of it but found herself wondering what she had done with her two years alone – her studies as a cunning woman had paused without her mother. She had taken up her mother's mantle, aware that she did not possess a quarter of her mother's knowledge. She had spent her time counselling the village folk when they were disposed to quarrel, fixing their troubles in love and looking into their futures, all the while with one eye on what lay beyond Thornton Cleveleys. But on the whole, she reminded herself, she was fortunate. Madoc was a loving, kind, clever companion, she had many friends, a valued role and a home she loved. Now matters of more immediate concern required her attention.

Tomorrow, she decided, she would speak to Wyot, the sheriff of Thornton Cleveleys, about Avery and his missing sister and seek his advice.

Chapter 2

Meryall had restuffed her mattress anew with herbs and sweet grasses in her vigorous spring cleaning, but despite this, her sleep was broken and filled with unsettling dreams. It was sometimes so after divination. She had continued to see fragments of her vision, but on waking, she could not recall more than brief images and this morning her dreams had left her with a grey, dragging weariness which she could not shake off.

As was her custom on a Thornton Cleveleys market day, Meryall rose early, while it was still dark. She had packed up her herbs, bottles and jars of salves, oils and powders into a large basket which she carried with woven straps across her shoulders. The weak, predawn brightness of the sky did nothing to improve her mood. The light had little strength and fog clung to the trees, folding a faint tang of the sea through the forest. Meryall hurried along the path, trying to chase away the cold and her mood.

The road to the village wove through the trees, before coming out on a path open to the sea, although the coast was just out of sight unless you walked a little way off the track over the damp, springy grasses. Meryall could hear the sea's gentle rush. Today, it seemed to be in an idle, unhurried mood. It too was blanketed beneath a thick mist.

Meryall often took a route down along the shore, but today she felt the need for cheerful bustle and companionship and was glad to hear the ringing cries of the stallholders as she reached the edge of the village.

The village square was already beginning to fill with traders, spreading their goods out on the stone steps of the hall and blankets and tables around the walls of the square. Meryall sighted a redhead and moved towards a handsome woman, her hair a bright spot in the dull day as she smiled and laughed with her customers. Katerin's warmth cheered her. She had been friends with her for many years, and they had shared a table at the market for at least the last ten. Katerin had already spread out her ribbons, threads and needles on her half of the stall. Meryall set down her pack and with a smile and kiss for Katerin began to put out her bundles of herbs and arrange the bottles and jars in neat rows around them.

The square rang with the mingled voices of traders singing out their wares, customers haggling and the clatter of wheels on the cobbles as farmers and villagers from nearby arrived in their carts to make purchases. Meryall waved to a trader who had set up a barrow of fresh fish. He was a flounder trampler – a fisherman who specialised in catching the large flatfish at the mouth of the river by treading the shallows, sensing the fish just below the surface of the mud with his feet and then spearing them quickly. Meryall was fond of the mild-flavoured flounder and wished she had not already set the evening meal to cook. The man made a brisk trade and quickly sold all of his fish.

Meryall saw a muscular man in his middle years, clad in a leather apron, heading towards the stall. She gave an inner sigh. The village smith was a frequent customer.

'How are you this morning, Aiden?' Meryall said.

'Not well, Mistress Meryall, not well at all!' he exclaimed.

Meryall made a noise of concern and encouraged him to elaborate with a wave of her hand.

'I argued with my neighbour yesterday, and today two horseshoes have already cracked as I was forging them. She has turned the eye upon me!'

Meryall knew Aiden's neighbour to be an elderly lady of uncertain temperament but doubted that she had done more than make a lewd hand gesture at Aiden. She patted him on the arm.

'I understand, Aiden. It is difficult when there is bad blood between neighbours.' She handed him a bundle of herbs. 'Burn half of this in your forge and the other half in your kitchen fire.' Meryall took several pretty dried herbs and bound them with an offcut of ribbon. 'And place this on your neighbour's front doorstep. You will find that all ill will is dissolved and that you will meet with a more favourable reception from her.'

Aiden took the items gratefully, giving Meryall a coin before hurrying off. Katerin was trying not to smile. When she was sure that Aiden was out of sight, she turned to Meryall.

'Did you just give Aiden a bouquet for his neighbour?'

Meryall feigned innocence. 'Magic takes many forms,' she replied.

Both she and Katerin saw good custom. Villagers stopped by Katerin's stall to buy a new ribbon or a packet of buttons and to buy herbs for peaceful sleep, a beauty charm, protective amulet or a poppet from Meryall's wares.

An hour or so before noon, they broke their fast, unpacking items from their bundles. Meryall took out a hard, pungent, grainy cheese, which she made from the milk of her goat, and a rough loaf of bread. Katerin pulled a jar of honey and a flask of ale from their wrappings and laid them out on a cloth on the stone step behind them. They sat at either end of the cloth and ate, keeping half an eye out for customers as they talked. Meryall told Katerin about her visit from Avery yesterday and asked Katerin if she would mind the stall for half an hour after lunch so that she could go and visit the sheriff to speak to him of the matter. Katerin agreed readily. A male voice hailed them from across the square and looking up, Meryall saw Katerin's husband, Randal, stride across the square. He stepped behind the table and dropped a kiss on Katerin's head, smiling and nodding to Meryall.

'I heard from my cousin, the woodsman, that a body was found in the forest last night, near the village of Lune,' Randal said.

'A girl?' Meryall asked sharply.

'No, a young man, with a wound in his stomach – too neat to be the work of an animal – more likely a narrow-bladed knife.'

Katerin shuddered. 'A terrible way to die, hurt and alone in the woods.'

Meryall closed her eyes for a moment, remembering her vision of Eda surrounded by armed men. She hoped that Avery had not run into trouble looking for her.

'Where have they taken the body?'

'To Madoc's apothecary shop.' Randall gestured up the road. 'Sheriff Wyot has requested that the body be examined, and an investigation made to try to trace his kinsfolk.'

Meryall nodded absently and stepped away to serve a customer who was browsing through her packets of herbs. She would visit Madoc's shop and view the body, she decided, before she spoke to Wyot.

By early afternoon, the traders were packing away and Katerin and Meryall, their packs light after the day's trade, separated at the edge of the square, with blessings to each other's loved ones and a parting embrace.

Meryall took the road away from the square and arrived after a short walk at a small house with the downstairs given over to the apothecary shop. She stood outside for a moment, looking at Madoc as he moved around the shop, grinding herbs in a huge stone mortar, then pouring the powder into a jar, before adding the next ingredient to be ground to the mortar. He was tall – well above the average height for a man – and strongly made, with dark hair touched with grey, and handsome features. A wave of love washed over her as she watched him work, but the sudden memory of the poor, lifeless body she knew lay in the shop brought a sobering surge of guilt. A bell tinkled as she pushed open the door and the deep smell of the apothecary's wares filled her nose. Madoc turned from his work, grinned at Meryall and stepped forward to greet her, arms held out. She met his embrace, enjoying his warmth and the clean scent of his skin. Meryall smiled up into his kind grey eyes for a moment, but then looked sombre.

'I heard that the sheriff had a corpse brought to you for examination?'

Madoc sighed, moving away to tidy bundles of spices and empty jars to make space on a seat for Meryall.

'Yes, a comely young man. It is a great shame. He has a rent in his lower abdomen and another in his upper thigh – knife wounds. The wound to the thigh would have bled freely, and I imagine that this was the wound that killed him. The wound to his stomach may have killed him eventually, with infection likely from such an injury, but not immediately.'

'Is there reason to believe that he had not lain long when found?' Meryall asked.

'The hunters who found him last night said that his body had not yet stiffened when they found him.'

Meryall hesitated a moment. 'Can I see him, please? I fear that I may know who he is.'

Madoc was startled but took Meryall's hand and walked with her to the back room of the shop, where he performed examinations and procedures. He had laid the body on his big scrubbed-oak work table, covered by a long piece of linen. He folded back the linen and invited Meryall to his side. Meryall looked down at Avery's fine-featured face, his dark eyes closed, lashes resting on his cheeks and his skin pale. She felt a deep sadness for this man – hardly more than a boy, who had sought her help. Madoc re-covered Avery's face and looked at Meryall with curiosity.

'It is as I thought,' she said. 'This is Avery Greenhalgh, the young man who visited me yesterday. He asked for help to find his missing sister. It does not seem to be a coincidence that he met so violent an end.' Meryall sighed deeply. She wished she had spoken to the sheriff sooner.

Madoc locked up the shop and walked with Meryall back to Horn Cottage. As they reached a fork in the path, Meryall took Madoc's hand. 'Do you mind if we walk along the shore for a little while? I feel in need of the freshness of the air today.'

Madoc agreed immediately, and they turned off, Madoc taking Meryall's pack from her as they scrambled down a rocky path to the beach. The sands stretched out for miles. This section was quiet. Near to the village, there were docks for the fisherman and for trading vessels to land, which made the beach lively with voices and the chink of rigging in the breeze, but here there was no one else in sight. Meryall put her arm through Madoc's, trying to let the scent of the sea and the power of the waves as they rolled against the rocks put her thoughts in order. They walked on until the afternoon light began to show tawny hints of pink, then returned to the path to the cottage.

Meryall had prepared root vegetables, herbs and some

dried meat from her stores that morning and put them to simmer in a stew for their evening meal. She hung the pot closer to the fire to set it bubbling to thicken the stock and put bread, butter and some more of her cheese on the table for them to eat as they talked and waited for their meal to be ready. Meryall took off her boots and put her feet into Madoc's lap as they sat close together in the warmth of the fire.

Madoc listened quietly to the details of Avery's visit and her vision. 'We should speak to Sheriff Allred,' he said.

Meryall rubbed her temples, feeling tight little muscles move under her fingers. 'I had planned to speak to him today because I feared for Avery's safety, but it appears I was too late. When he comes to you for your report on the cause of death tomorrow morning, tell him to drop by to see me, and I will tell him all that I know.'

'Yes, there is no point disturbing him tonight – nothing can be done until it is light.'

Meryall murmured her agreement, yet her thoughts turned to Eda again and again as she remembered the small, delicate face within the dark folds of the cloak she had glimpsed in her vision.

After their meal, Meryall poured small cups of parsnip wine for them both. Meryall was well known for her skill in making this pleasant, light golden drink with parsnips that had been sweetened by the frost. Madoc sipped appreciatively at his wine and took Meryall's hand in his, stroking her fingers. The taste of parsnip wine often roused memories of his travels in Spain and Madoc would tell Meryall tales of the city of Jerez de la Frontera, home of the famed sweet sherry and a maze of narrow streets, enclosed by ancient walls. Madoc had travelled widely in his youth, seeking knowledge of medicine and plants in distant corners of the world and working as ship's apothecary to pay for his passage, before returning to the village to establish his apothecary shop. Meryall loved to hear his stories of sea storms, thundersnow, intrigue and mystery. It gave her pleasure to imagine the quiet, measured, wise man she knew on such dangerous and exciting adventures. Meryall turned over Madoc's left hand and passed her thumb over the tattooed mark there. She had asked him about it many times, but he always declined to explain it, saying with a laugh that he would tell her the story of how he got the mark one day when she had leisure enough for a very long tale. Meryall turned the little cup in her hand. The cups had been a gift from Madoc – he had requested that a merchant friend of his, Jura, find for him the type of cups they had seen some years ago on their travels, knowing that Meryall would be enchanted with the pure, bright colour. After much searching, Jura had purchased them from a market in Constantinople, delivering them to Madoc's shop with a smile of triumph. The pottery was remarkably fine. They were glazed in a bright blue, with a pattern of interlinked stylised flowers picked out in white. Meryall was fond of them. Madoc had told her that the bright blue matched the colour of the sky in that sunlit, faraway place and that the cups were of the kind used in the stalls that sold the dark, fragrant brew made from the bitter beans that the Ottoman people so loved. She asked him to tell her again about the bazaars he had seen there, and they filled the evening with stories and talk of the fashions, food, people and places he had seen.

Madoc's own living quarters were above his shop, and Meryall sometimes stayed there, too, but preferred the greater comfort and amenities of her own home. They both appreciated their separate space, however, and so kept their two dwellings. Besides, Meryall disliked the spiders and other creatures that dropped out of the thatched roof. Not that she minded the creatures themselves, but she did not relish them falling onto the bed canopy or landing in her shoes during the night. The cave house did not have this problem.

Meryall had heard that elsewhere in Europe, relationships between men and women were not tolerated outside of wedlock, but here, the Christian missionaries and emissaries of the Roman Church had found only limited interest amongst the people, who predominantly adhered to the old ways. There were some, like Katerin and Randal, who chose to celebrate a hand-fasting and to live together, or who lived together for convenience, but no one in the village had misgivings about anyone who chose to be lovers but not live under one roof. Meryall looked up at the little carved figure of the goddess in her aspect as mother, full-figured and smiling, on her dresser, and said a silent prayer of gratitude that their way of life was so filled with joy and wisdom.

Chapter 3

The morning dawned bright and crisp. The thick stone walls of the cottage were illuminated by cheerful sunshine when Meryall awoke. She lay looking up at the curved stone ceiling above her, thinking about the tasks that needed to be attended to that day. Meryall was glad of the brightness, after the fog of the previous day. Madoc had left early to open the shop. He had put the kettle on the warming plate of the stove and laid out the tisane things for her. Meryall smiled as she poured the water. Madoc had filled the pot with his favoured combination of herbs for the morning – peppermint, rosemary and hyssop and the clean, fresh smell filled the kitchen. Meryall warmed her hands around her cup and breathed the scent of the herbs deeply.

Stretching, Meryall rose and took ground oats from her store, mixing them with water from her pitcher, salt and a large spoonful of melted bacon fat. She kneaded the rough dough and shaped it into a flat circle, scored twice, crossways, with her knife. Wheat was not common this far north, and most local bread was made from oats or barley. Although the traders brought wheat flour with them, this was mainly the preserve of higher tables than Meryall's. From long experience, the round of dough fitted neatly into the heavy iron girdle, and Meryall placed it over the coals. The bannock bread soon began to give forth fragrant steam as it browned in the heat. Meryall turned the bread over and set out cheese and butter on the table while the bread finished cooking. She took the bannock out of the pan and set it to cool, cutting out a farl to eat for her breakfast. The rest would be used for a midday meal, or perhaps eaten with a stew for supper.

Meryall had cleaned and tidied the kitchen and had set about the task of cleaning jars, ready for a batch of her sleep salve when she heard a smart knock at the door. Sheriff Wyot Allred threw it open and was about to call out to Meryall, when he noticed her and smiled, coming forward to plant a kiss on her cheek, before seating himself at the table without ceremony.

'Well, Meryall, I hear that you have the key to the mystery of this poor dead boy we have on our hands?' The sheriff was a heavyset man, with broad chest and shoulders and a rounded belly. He possessed such a sweet-natured countenance that Meryall could not help but find his bright eyes and ready smile appealing – and she knew that many women in the village were partial to Wyot's company, although he was too honest and honourable to entangle himself with more than one woman at a time. When she was a girl, Meryall too had been charmed by the big man's laugh and twinkling eyes. There had been a kiss exchanged under the light of a harvest moon, but they had long since settled into a comfortable friendship.

Meryall took out a flask of parsnip wine and poured Wyot a small measure.

'No, Wyot, indeed I wish that was the case. I can, however, tell you his name and about his visit to me on the day he died.'

Wyot sat back and awaited Meryall's account. He had often visited her before when a problematic case had presented itself. Her skill in divination and her common sense was of much value to him, and Wyot was a man who knew well how to make use of the knowledge of those around him. Meryall had found this to be a rare ability in men of his profession and valued him, in turn, for he was fair and vigorous in the discharge of his duties.

As Meryall gave him her update, Wyot's expression grew increasingly serious.

'I know the lord of the castle – Edward De Lune. His family are of an ancient, noble line. But Edward has had a reputation for sharp dealings, in business, in his relationships with women and his gaming. I am most concerned to hear of the disappearance of a young woman in his service. Indeed, I have heard rumours of young women vanishing from the castle before, but there has never been enough evidence to pursue an investigation – and the other young women had no family to make a fuss about their disappearance.'

'We must do something, Wyot … she might be in need of our aid.' Meryall's stomach felt cold with fear.

'Can you divine anything further about where this girl is to be found?' Wyot asked.

'I can try,' Meryall replied. She thought for a moment and drew from her drawer a disk of polished brass, which she set down on the table. She pulled the window shade half closed, refilled Wyot's cup, put the flask by his elbow and sat down in front of the mirror. Meryall drew deep breaths, focusing on the image of Eda as she had last seen her, holding her face in her mind as she looked far into the mirror. Beyond the surface, she saw a shadow growing, swirling and changing shape until it formed the image of a path. The path was deep within a forest, and Meryall heard in her mind the ring of horses' hooves treading the path.

Meryall concentrated on drawing nearer to the sound and saw the outline of three riders. Moving over the group, she saw a cloaked shape held against the chest of one of them – a man. Looking keenly at the small form, Meryall saw a little, pale hand and locks of dark, curled hair showing from beneath the raised hood of the fur-lined cloak. The hand moved within the warmth of the fur, disappearing from view. Meryall focused her vision on the road ahead and saw the outline of a twin-towered castle against the horizon. She pulled her consciousness back, and the castle faded back into a mist that soon cleared to leave only the reflection of her own tired green eyes and pale skin.

Wyot listened to Meryall's report of her scrying. He sat still in his chair with his glance fixed on the floor but his head tilted towards her. At the mention of the castle, he rubbed his hand to his face, meeting her eye. 'You are describing Lune Castle, Meryall. I can only think that they must have taken her back there, surmising that now her brother has been killed, there will be no one else to come looking for her.'

'What will you do?' Meryall asked.

'It is difficult to know how to proceed.' Wyot looked drawn and sad. 'De Lune is a powerful man, I cannot search his castle without strong proof and–' he looked at her apologetically '–although the results of your divination have given me every proof I have needed, time and time again...' He shrugged, leaving his sentence unfinished.

'Your vision has given me a good lead which may help a skilled tracker to find the proof we need to gain a warrant from the court, however.'

Meryall leaned forward and grasped his arm. 'Don't send your tracker alone, Wyot... I fear for the safety of anyone seeking Eda.'

Chapter 4

Avarall and Everett left their horses with their bridles caught in the bushes to graze happily in a patch of grass by a clear running burn, near to where the sheriff had told them to start looking for signs of three horses and any indicators of a struggle, or of a young woman. The horses were strong and well-conditioned, and they had made good time. The stretches of smooth, clear road had enabled them to increase their pace, but even so, they had a good ride ahead of them to reach home before dark and no time to waste in their investigations.

Avarall and Everett had served together for a long time and quickly found a working rhythm, communicating efficiently with a gesture or a word. Both wore soft boots which made little noise and disturbed the ground less than their usual heavy footwear. Avarall had strung her yew bow across her shoulders, and both she and Everett carried a dagger at the waist. Wyot had been clear in communicating Meryall's warning and was keen that they proceed cautiously and not place themselves in danger.

Avarall ran her eyes over the trail, walking softly at the edge of the path to avoid obscuring the tracks with her footprints. Everett followed on the other side of the path, his eyes scanning the undergrowth. Avarall's fair and Everett's dark bowed heads moved in tandem along the track, eyes focused on the ground. They soon picked up the traces of three horses – the shoes were distinctively styled, and the size varied, with two smaller prints and one larger set, which Avarall guessed had come from a war charger. They walked on for some time, tracing the tracks. Everett stopped, signalling for Avarall to join him. Several snapped blackthorn twigs marked a point in the trail where footsteps also began to accompany the horse tracks.

'It looks like someone slid from a horse here,' Everett said, pointing to a heavier set of imprints, made by a small foot – a woman or child's boot, partly obscured by a larger footprint which looked around the size of a grown man's boot.

'And here it seems like they were followed,' Avarall added. She looked closely at the thorn bush and carefully pulled at something caught in the sharp barbs. They both inspected the object – it was a fine thread of wool, and it looked as if someone had fallen against the bush and caught their clothing as they pulled away. 'Whoever this woman or child was, from the footprints it looks as though they sought to run from the horsemen, caught their garment on the thorns and tried to free themselves to escape.'

They inspected the tracks.

'The footprints are unclear, from much coming and

going,' Avarall said, 'but it appears that from here, all of the party were once again back on their horses.'

Everett frowned. 'That suggests that they recaptured their prey, one way or another, as there are no footprints ahead on this trail, only horse tracks from here.'

'Unless the escapee succeeded in taking a horse,' Avarall added, with a smile. 'But then the men would be one horse short, would they not?'

Everett looked unconvinced.

'Two of the men could then have mounted one horse so that they could all pursue their quarry...' Avarall continued, her eager eyes seeking answers in the tracks.

Everett hesitated. 'I wish that were so, Ava ... but look here, further down the track, the horse tracks are as they were before. If one horse were by this point carrying a much larger burden and one a lighter load, we could see that in how heavily the hooves of the horses were marking the path.'

Avarall sighed. 'Well, perhaps it is as you say, but I like not to think of this poor woman or child taken up again, against their will.' She frowned, kneeling next to the largest set of tracks. 'Do you not think that the tracks of the large horse are deeper here?' she said.

Everett knelt beside her, his fingers tracing the indentations in the earth. He shrugged and walked over to look at the tracks of the other two horses. 'One of the horses' tracks look a little lighter ... it is possible that two rode the war charger and this horse bore no rider.'

Avarall sighed. She had been hoping for proof that Eda had escaped, but here it looked more like she had transferred to another horse. Carried tied pillion, perhaps, after her attempt to escape.

They continued working until dusk, tracing the tracks to the edge of the path which ran to the gates of Lune Castle, before turning back and returning to their horses, heading back into Thornton Cleveleys in the fading light.

Returning their horses to the stables in the keep, they walked up to the sheriff's great hall, tired and hungry after their meticulous search. A fire blazed in the large fireplaces at either end of the hall. Although it was early spring, the air was still crisp in the evenings, and Avarall and Everett were grateful for the warmth and cheerfulness of the flames. A man came forward to greet them, showing them to seats within the nook of the fireplace and bringing them a jug of mead and bowls of broth, rich with herbs and filled with vegetables and strands of meat. He added a loaf of bread and some apples and cheese to their meal. They thanked him and set about the food and drink with vigour. They had eaten their fill and were sitting back with their dusty boots against the hearth and their mead cups in their hands, talking over their day's work when Wyot joined them, drawing a chair from the long table in the centre of the hall to the fire and taking a seat between them.

Avarall handed him the fine thread of wool she had wrapped in a scrap of leather in the purse at her waist. Wyot sat listening intently to their report, turning the soft threads over and over in his fingers.

'Thank you for your work. You deserve a good rest after your efforts,' Wyot said with a nod.

Avarall and Everett rose, bowed and turned to leave.

Glancing over her shoulder as she opened the heavy door, Avarall saw that Wyot sat deep in thought, a trace of a frown shadowing his features. She shook her head softly. They had done all that they could, yet she feared it was not enough.

Wyot sat alone in the hall until the fire began to fade, the creeping chill of the evening rousing him from his reverie. Avarall and Everett were exceptional trackers and had done well, yet he was hugely frustrated. Their evidence suggested that Meryall was right – Eda was being held against her will in the castle, but it was not enough evidence to take forward a request for a warrant to search Lord De Lune's property and to question him about Eda. The town magistrate, who must grant a permit for an investigation in a case of this nature, before it could be considered by the court, was a fair-minded and meticulous man. Although he would not be cowed by Lord De Lune's riches or reputation, he would require a reasonable level of proof before he was willing to give consent for an investigation. Eda had no living relatives to raise a complaint; they had no evidence that she was not still alive and there was no evidence to link Lord De Lune or his men to her brother's death. He would have to think carefully about how he could pursue this investigation – informally, for now.

Wyot called for a quill, ink and parchment and sat long in thought composing a note. Sealing it, he sent a boy out to Horn Cottage, equipped with a horn lantern to light his way along the dark path through the woods.

Chapter 5

The fire burned brightly in the hearth and bathed Horn Cottage in a cheerful glow. The blaze cast the rough surfaces of the whitewashed walls into relief, making the old carvings seem to dance and move in the light.

The evening had been pleasant. After a long, busy day, Madoc had arrived at Horn Cottage bearing a pack full of mysterious packages, wrapped in linen and parchment, some with words and lettering that was unfamiliar to Meryall, despite her respectable knowledge of languages. He had been visited by an old friend of his – Jura, a merchant whom he had sailed with some years ago, passing through on his way to Lune and breaking his journey to take a midday meal with Madoc. Jura had brought gifts of spices and wine, as well as news of the adventures and misadventures of their acquaintances.

They unwrapped the parcels – unpicking knots in yarn drawn tight by the salt air of a long sea voyage, slicing through linen tape bleached by the faraway sun and carefully folding up the cloth and wrapping papers for future use. A variety of bottles, wooden boxes and books lay before them, tempting them away from the meal that awaited them, bubbling patiently on the hotplate.

Madoc selected a bottle of wine and warmed it in a jug by the hearth, adding a pinch or two of spices from the fragrant, ornately carved boxes laid out like coffers of jewels on the plain, scrubbed-oak table. He poured warm, spiced wine into Meryall's cup. Meryall inhaled deeply. The rich claret mingled well with the exotic scent of cinnamon and cloves.

'There is trouble between the Spanish and the Buccaneers of Hispaniola, I am told,' Madoc mused as he turned his wine cup between his palms. 'The seas are beset with greedy profiteers, though being so vast, I suppose it is easy enough to choose a stretch of ocean untroubled by such things for one's travels.'

Meryall smiled. 'Our own people are not unknown to seek profits overseas, Madoc.'

'Indeed,' Madoc acknowledged with a gracious nod, 'but our trade has always been based on diplomacy and relationships, rather than aggression and subjugation.'

'But for how long? The influence of our neighbours – with their excuse of Christian zealotry may leave us without trade routes if we continue as we are now.'

Madoc sighed. 'I cannot believe that our parliament of chiefs would allow us to pursue such methods. The draw of our universities and our advanced knowledge of languages, arts and navigation have always been enough to trade upon thus far.'

'And long may it be so,' Meryall replied solemnly. They touched their cups in a toast. 'And did your merchant friend mention to you whether he has dealings with Lord De Lune?' Meryall asked, her conversation with Wyot and concern for Eda at the front of her mind.

'Yes, indeed, it appears there will be few merchants unfamiliar with Lord De Lune. He is perhaps the most vigorous and influential trader in our region. Jura talks of him as a clever and ruthless dealer. He drives a hard bargain for the goods he buys and pays less for them than any man in the country. He buys such large quantities that the merchants are willing to accept a smaller price per measure, due to the surety of him buying all of their stock, thus saving them the trouble and cost of travelling around to different purchasers.'

Meryall rolled her eyes. 'And I am sure that Lord De Lune sells his goods on at an excellent profit.'

Madoc gave a wry smile. 'He keeps his prices competitive, of course, but there is little doubt that he is able to turn a fine profit.'

Meryall had hoped for some more salacious gossip about Lord De Lune's dealings with women, but supposed that Jura's interest would be solely in mercantile affairs. She turned the conversation, teasingly, to Jura's appearance.

'Does Jura still wear that gold and pearl earring you told me of? He must look most piratical!'

Madoc smiled. 'Indeed he does. I have requested that he bring me a matching one and pierces it through my ear on his next visit, so much do I like it.'

Meryall laughed, taking Madoc's face in her hands and kissing him. 'Handsome as you are, you need no adornment … however, I confess, I would rather enjoy seeing such a bauble in your ear.'

Draining the last sips of her wine, Meryall stood to prepare their supper – oat bread, cheese and fragrant slices of apple – some of the last from her barrel – and a steaming bowl of broth. She arranged the plates to her liking and carried them to the table. Placing them down, she jumped at a sudden knock at the door. It was late in the evening. She looked over at Madoc, who raised an eyebrow inquiringly before rising and opening the front door. A ruddy, plump-cheeked boy stood on the doorstep, holding a rolled and sealed scroll of parchment in one hand and a horn lantern in the other. Meryall recognised him as one of Wyot's stable boys.

'Come in, lad, it is cold out there. What brings you to us at such a late hour?' Madoc said, gently steering the boy by the shoulders to stand before the fire and taking the scroll from him.

'The sheriff asked that I bring you this scroll as soon as possible,' he replied.

Meryall grinned. 'And did the sheriff promise you a reward for your services?'

The boy beamed and jiggled a pouch at his belt. It gave the merry jingle of coins. Meryall grinned. Wyot was a generous man. 'Well, we will add some supper to your payment, by way of thanks for your diligence in delivering your message on a cold, dark night.'

The boy stepped away cheerfully with a piece of Meryall's cheese and some oat bread for his supper in his waist pouch, leaving them to read the sheriff's note.

Meryall passed Madoc a knife, and he slid it under the seal, unrolling the parchment and pinning it flat on the table with their wine cups so that they could both read the large, looping handwriting that filled the page. It contained a request for their services so unusual that they both sat in silence for some time reading and rereading the message before they were able to meet each other's eyes and begin to discuss the matter.

They talked over his proposal for much of the night and eventually agreed that they would accept. The new dawn would bring much to do. The sheriff had requested their presence early the next morning to commence their mission.

Chapter 6

It was still dark when they arose and began to make preparations for their journey. Madoc had added his herbs, jars and bottles to Meryall's bundle, along with clothing and toiletry items. Meryall took the scraps of oat bread left in the pantry out for the birds and locked the cottage door. Madoc hefted the pack onto his back, and they walked into the village in silence, their thoughts on the task ahead of them.

The morning sun gave a little warmth as they took the path into Thornton Cleveleys. They could hear the sea, although it was not within sight of the track and Meryall traced the salty tang of the waves in the air. Today, she knew, the women and children would be out on the shore, raking the sands in search of cockles and clams.

Wyot met them at the door of the great hall, gesturing them to the long table at the centre, where there were places set for a morning meal. 'I am glad you decided to come. Please come in and eat with us,' he said, shaking Madoc's hand and folding Meryall in a brief but firm hug. The servant was ladling porridge into bowls for them as they approached a table generously laid with cold meats, cheeses, fruit and honey. Meryall added some honey to her bowl of porridge and poured a cup of new milk from the big rough jug. Wyot waited patiently for the servant to withdraw, smiling at him and nodding his thanks. 'I am grateful to you both for agreeing to undertake this task – it is not without risk, and yet I do not know how else we can proceed,' Wyot said. 'I have a kinsman, Faron Allred, whose wife Aelcea is sick. Aelcea is a cousin of Lord De Lune and was a favourite of his late mother. Their quarters are within the walls of the castle. I have written to him to suggest that you both undertake a thorough examination and treatment of her. We know not whether it is her body or her spirit that ails her and so I have good cause to send you both. As you know, while this is a genuine need, I am hoping that placing you both within the castle for a few days will enable you to gather information about Eda's disappearance. Faron will make you most welcome. He is at once grateful for your help and aware of the dual reasons for your presence in the castle. His staff will ensure that you have assistance in asking what questions you will and going where you wish.' Wyot hesitated. 'I scarcely need to remind you that you must take great care of yourselves and watch over one another.'

Madoc drew back his cloak to show the handle of a blade. 'Meryall and I have our knives in our belts. We are well aware of the need to go carefully within the castle.' 'How can we get messages back to you if we need to?' he added.

Wyot drew his chair back from the table and stepped

over to the door, calling to someone in the outer hall. In a few moments, a fair-haired young woman, in leather riding breeches and a tunic with the red chevron of the sheriff's arms on the breast, entered the room, walking confidently across to the table.

'Avarall, I dare say you know our apothecary, Madoc, and Mistress Meryall of Horn Cottage?'

'Indeed!' Avarall laughed. 'Who in the village has not had need of Meryall's charms and scrying and Madoc's remedies?'

'Avarall is a fine tracker and a sound shot with a bow,' Wyot said. 'She will go with you and will stay within my kinsfolk's quarters with you. She will be able to return here swiftly if you need to get a message to me.'

Wyot pulled out a chair for Avarall and invited her to eat with them. They went over the details of the plan. Avarall showed a sharpness of mind that impressed Meryall and Madoc and lessened their worries about their trip. She gave an in-depth description of the layout of the castle, which she had gained information about from her fellows amongst the sheriff's staff. Lune Castle was considered to be an excellent place to work, although Lord De Lune was rumoured to be an exacting man. It had a large number of subterranean stores, which ran beneath the main buildings. Lord De Lune had a reputation as a charming but untrustworthy man. He had increased the wealth of his estate through much trading and industry, but there was some reluctance amongst some of his neighbours to deal with him, as he had shown himself to be ruthless in his pursuit of profit. As they knew, there had been murmurings about the disappearance of women in his household previously. She had heard from an elder living within the sheriff's keep, who recalled having been told by a relative who resided at the castle that a young woman of the household had previously been rumoured to be involved in a dalliance with Lord De Lune and had later disappeared without a trace. Avarall had been able to find out little more than this vague information. Meryall was amused to notice that despite delivering her report in detail, Avarall had eaten well of the cheese and bread and continued her talk as she refilled her porridge bowl at the cauldron on the fireplace. Smiling, Meryall refilled the young woman's cup as she talked on with enthusiasm about her findings.

'There is an apothecary within the town walls,' Avarall said, turning to Madoc, 'so you may need to be sensitive to his feelings. He has been treating Mistress Aelcea for some time without success and so may feel threatened by your presence.'

Madoc acknowledged her point with a nod, adding, 'We will do well to seek him out soon after our arrival, as a mark of respect.'

Their meal finished, the party said their goodbyes, with Avarall going ahead to the stables to collect the horses that she had ordered to be made ready for their departure. Wyot pressed a bag of coins into their hands for the expenses of their journey and stay at the castle and wished them success. The air outside was fresh, and the sun shone brightly, making the prospect of a ride through the woods and on to the green valley along the banks of the River Lune seem enjoyable, despite the seriousness of their mission.

At the stables, Avarall and Everett had readied the horses, who stood patiently waiting for their passengers. Everett took the pack from Madoc and secured it to the saddle of a handsome Dales pony. The pony was black, sturdy and strong with silken tufts at his fetlocks and a thick, shining mane. Meryall's own pony was the same breed, but a pretty reddish-brown bay, and Avarall's another black pony, a hand or so smaller than Madoc's. Meryall praised the ponies. She knew the sheriff took pride in his Dales ponies, raised on the land he held to the north of the village. The ponies were well known for their steady nature and endurance. Meryall was pleased to be riding again, as she rarely had the opportunity to do so.

The journey was pleasant – they forded the River Wyre, then the road took them away from the coast and through the gentle countryside, studded with villages and hamlets. The sun continued to shine, and the many birds which dwelt along the banks of the little tributaries of the rivers of Wyre and Lune added cheer to their ride, wheeling and calling above the water. At last, they caught a glimpse of the River Lune and moved along the road to follow its shining crescent as it wound through the valley. There were few houses along its banks, but they were able to sight fishermen here and there, and as they drew close to the outskirts of the town of Lune, they saw a group of children playing in the shallows, splashing and laughing as they ran in and out of the water.

The castle cast an imposing shadow on the town at its feet. The twin-towered grey stone facade loomed grim and uncompromising over the streets. However, the lanes at the base of the hill which led up to the gates rang with lively calls from shopkeepers and stallholders, and there was a bustle and busyness which gave an impression of prosperity.

Avarall guided them through the noisy press of the crowds and on to the gates. Meryall noticed that throughout the seemingly well-kept and thriving town were many ragged figures moving amongst the masses. Beggars missing eyes and limbs haunted the entrances to alleys and doorways, pushed into the margins of the crowd. It made her sad to see such poverty and hunger amidst the plenty of the town.

The gates were open, and inside the main courtyard, market stalls ran all around the walls, with merchants selling fine silks, wines and jewellery. The smell of spices filled the air and Meryall could see Madoc's eye eagerly seeking the stalls selling rare and exotic resins and spice. Madoc had grown familiar with many of these on his travels but rarely had the opportunity to replenish his supplies. Meryall favoured her native herbs on the whole for her work, although she enjoyed the flavour of spice in wines and food.

'Lord De Lune is renowned for his links with merchants from abroad,' Avarall said. 'His market days are well known for attracting the most expensive and unusual goods – many wealthy people come, and there is usually a feast afterwards in the great hall. Lord De Lune takes a commission from all of these stallholders and makes a good deal of profit.'

Meryall looked curiously at the merchants and their wares. Brightly coloured silks, brocades and velvets caught Meryall's eye, amongst stands displaying delicate necklaces, earrings and bracelets. These, she noticed, were discreetly flanked by tough-looking men, who loitered while their obsequious masters traded with finely dressed men and ladies.

They walked to the left wing of the inner courtyard and Avarall rapped on a heavy oak door in the stone wall. A servant answered, glanced at the red chevron on Avarall's tunic and waved them into a stone-flagged hallway. They entered and climbed a set of narrow stairs behind the serving girl, who opened a door at the top of the stairs, which gave into a pleasant room with windows overlooking the market below and colourful tapestries upon the walls. A fire burned in the grate, the fire flanked by comfortable chairs. A stocky man stood to welcome them in. They could see his likeness to Wyot, with the same cheerful fine eyes and warm smile. 'You must be Faron Allred.' Meryall smiled. 'You are very much like Wyot.'

'Mistress Meryall and Master Madoc!' he replied. 'Indeed, it is an honour to see you, although I am sorry it is not in happier circumstances, upon every account.' Meryall could see the effort it took for Faron to greet them with warmth and energy; his tiredness surrounded him like a cloak and Meryall felt it roll off him in heavy waves.

'Please do not trouble yourself in attending to us, Faron,' she said. 'We are most aware that we come at a time of grave difficulty for you. How is your wife today?'

'She is much the same,' he replied with a sigh, gratefully touching Meryall's arm and gesturing for them all to be seated. 'She sleeps continually and is so weak when she wakes that she can scarcely talk. Our apothecary, Richard Mangnall, has made such efforts to effect a cure, but his remedies have been to no avail.'

'We would like to meet with Master Mangnall,' Madoc said. 'It would be most useful to hear from him what has already been tried. Do you think he would be amenable to meeting with us today?'

'Indeed, I believe he will be, but please, allow my servant to settle you in your quarters before you seek him out. She has prepared refreshments and water for washing for you.' Faron rose and went to the door, calling out to the serving girl, who entered the room quickly and conducted them along the corridor to a good-sized room looking out on the river as it curved away beneath them. It was furnished with a big feather bed, canopied with heavy curtains, a table and chairs in front of the fireplace and a stand holding a steaming basin of water and cloths for drying themselves. Avarall had followed the serving girl on up to a bedchamber in the attic.

Madoc poured ale into the cups awaiting them on the table and sat while Meryall washed her face and hands in the basin, before washing himself. Refreshed, they sat with their ale, picking at the dried fruits and cheeses that were laid out for them as they talked easily about their journey. Though aware of the seriousness of their task, there was freshness and novelty in the business of it that brought a sense of momentum and energy to them both. Meryall glanced out of the window – it was near midday. They changed out of their heavy, dusty travelling clothes. Meryall shrugged on a clean, light gown. The linen fitted loosely, and the softness of the well-worn dress was pleasant against her skin. She felt the tell-tale dawning ache in her muscles that told her that without proper treatment, she would find sitting and walking a chore by the following morning.

Madoc and Meryall assisted one another in applying a pungent balm to stimulate the circulation to their sore muscles and then, feeling the spreading warmth of the healing herbs, went to call for Avarall, who was to show them the way to the apothecary's shop.

Chapter 7

Avarall led them out of the main gates, down into the town and along the main street, crowded with horses, carriages, carts, people and much muck from the presence of such. Near the centre, they found an ample, imposing shopfront graced with a sign showing a pestle and mortar. Peering through the window, Meryall could see ornate shelves crowded with bottles, jars and packages. Inside, it was oppressively warm, with the heat of a fire augmented by the heat of a small brazier warming a complicated copper still. As in Madoc's shop (and indeed her own), the air was thick with the scent of herbs, but here, the many bottles and closely packed shelves, with each item labelled in a sparse, narrow hand, felt unwelcoming to Meryall. She could not say why the atmosphere of the shop oppressed her but found herself longing to leave the dark, cramped space. Madoc looked about with interest before ringing the bell upon the counter. A tall, spare man, young in appearance, but with a sallow skin which deprived his features of any freshness, entered from the back room, wiping his hands on the apron about his waist. Madoc stepped forward with a smile and held out his hand to the young man. 'I am Madoc Riley, apothecary of Thornton Cleveleys. I am pleased to make your acquaintance, Richard of Lune.'

Richard took his hand and shook it firmly, before turning to Meryall. 'And Mistress Meryall?' he said, politely holding his hand out to her. 'It is much to our great misfortune that we have no cunning man or woman to serve our village,' Richard told her, 'so I am pleased to see you both here to help with the care of Mistress Allred. The gods know that I have made little progress with her.'

They were both relieved by this warm welcome. Meryall too had been unsure of her reception. Madoc was generous in acknowledging where the limits of his medicines lay and where the need for Meryall's knowledge began, but she had found that many apothecaries were dismissive of the art of the cunning folk and held their own medicines in high esteem.

'Please,' Madoc began, 'tell us what remedies you have trialled in her care.'

The two apothecaries sat down to an earnest and detailed discussion. Avarall had gone to check on the horses, and after a short time, Meryall felt the draw of the beautiful things she had seen earlier on and stood at the window, trying to look up into the courtyard at the end of the road to watch the rich buyers and richer merchants going about their business.

Looking on, she saw a black-haired man, finely attired in a cloak of red and gold over a black tunic and hose. He went from stall to stall, smiling and stopping to admire a jewel or a piece of cloth and to exchange pleasantries with the merchants. He was shadowed by two burly men-at-arms, who, in turn, exchanged curt nods with the guards accompanying the stallholders.

Meryall watched him for some time and noted that although the stallholders greeted him with gracious smiles, there was a hesitancy in the way they moved in his presence that made her feel that they were wary of him.

Madoc and Richard were looking grave. She joined them at the table.

'I think perhaps that Mistress Allred has a malady of the spirit,' Richard said. 'She has not responded to the treatments that I have administered – I have given herbs to bring her to wakefulness, stimulants to enliven her mind and her appetite, yet she remains so fatigued that she is hard put to form words when she does awaken.'

Meryall tapped the table thoughtfully with her fingers. 'Is there reason to believe that she has suffered any loss or sadness that would have reduced her spirits so?'

'None that is known to her husband – and weak as she is, she has not been able to name any wrong or worry herself… I grow concerned that her muscles will begin to waste and she is losing weight quickly because we are unable to induce her to eat. Thanks be that we are able to feed her fluids, by trickling water or honeyed wine into her mouth with a sponge.'

'We will visit her later and see what we can make of her. Will you come with us?' Madoc said.

'If you are willing, I would be honoured to watch you make your examinations,' Richard replied.

Avarall walked behind Meryall and Madoc, alert and quick-eyed, as they made their way back through the town to their quarters. The sun was low behind them, and they found that their stomachs were keenly reminding them that some hours had passed since they last ate. The servant guided them to the hall where Faron had greeted them earlier and seated them with jugs of water and ale and a plate of fruit to await dinner. Faron, they were told, was sitting with his wife, talking and reading to her in the hopes of comforting and stimulating her in her fatigue and distress. They sat and talked over their day for a while, discussing the remedies that Richard had already trialled in Aelcea Allred's care and making hypotheses about what might be causing her illness and how they might alleviate it. Meryall favoured a depression of spirit, possibly precipitated by a shock or loss and Madoc wondered about a sickness of the blood, perhaps due to loss of blood, a diet lacking in nourishing meats and vegetables or even parasitic infestation. Avarall recalled that an aunt of hers had sickened and died after a similar illness, brought on by a blow to the head. Faron arrived as the doors were opened to bring in their meal. The servants carried in platters of sea trout, freshly fished from the River Lune where they had started to return to spawn, which lay on a bed of boiled wild garlic and nettle tips; hard cheeses and cheese curds, bread, pale creamy butter and a dish of wood pigeon stuffed with dried apricots and finely chopped pork.

They ate and chatted easily – although Faron still appeared tired and low in spirits, he continued to make an effort to be hospitable and to listen and converse with interest. After they had eaten, they retired to the fire with cups of mead.

Madoc enquired whether they might examine Aelcea and Faron was eager in arranging for this to happen, dispatching a servant to ensure that Aelcea was helped to sit up and change her nightdress if she wished to, and sending word to the apothecary of Lune that an examination would take place imminently. The servant returned and confirmed that they might visit Aelcea in her chamber, but that Master Richard was busy with surgery and begged that they continue without him. Meryall and Madoc collected items they felt they might need in making their examination and followed the servant down the corridor.

The bedroom was large and pleasant, with the same attractive views over the country that Meryall had admired in her quarters. The curtains around the bed were open, and a slim, handsome woman with light brown hair and hazel eyes sat propped up with pillows. She had violet shadows under her eyes, and her skin was pale, almost bluish. The effort of smiling and raising her hand in greeting appeared to drain her of energy, momentarily, and she sat still, her hands on her lap, and her eyes cast down. Meryall approached the bed and explained her and Madoc's presence and desire to assist in her treatment. Faron had agreed that it might be best if they saw Aelcea alone for her examination unless she particularly wished her husband to be present.

Meryall found it easier to work with fewer distractions.

Aelcea inclined her head to indicate her understanding and looked into Meryall's eyes with great intensity before her eyes shut against her will and her head drooped back against her pillows. Madoc stepped forward and checked her pulse. It was slow and faint against his fingers, and her skin felt chilled. Madoc pushed Aelcea's hair from her face with care and raised her eyelid. The rims of her eyes were also pale. Her lids fluttered, and she opened her eyes, looking up at Madoc and sighing as she closed her eyes, her breathing shallow and a little ragged.

Meryall sat on the edge of the bed and took Aelcea's hand. She closed her eyes and used her inner sight to see and feel the person before her. Aelcea's presence grew before her like a bright outline. She could feel that Aelcea was deeply tired, her energy low and her spirit depressed by fear and a weakness that felt like a dense fog about her. Meryall called to Aelcea's higher self – the part of her that dwelt beyond the body and was unaffected by its troubles. Aelcea's essence filled her mind – lightness and gentleness flooding through Meryall. Aelcea's higher self showed her an image of a small red pot, held in her hands. Aelcea closed her hands around the pot and then reopened them, empty. She smiled at Meryall and pulled back her energy, leaving Meryall alone once more, in the strange space between minds.

Meryall opened her eyes. Aelcea appeared to be sleeping peacefully now, and Madoc was seated on a chair by the window, watching them with patient interest. Seeing Meryall open her eyes, he stood and came to embrace her, aware that she sometimes felt disorientated for a few moments when she returned from a journey of this nature.

Her head now clear, Meryall walked to a table furnished with a mirror and looked amongst the items there. Aelcea had an ornate silver mirror and comb set and a selection of bottles, jars of pomades and perfumes. Meryall sorted through them until she found a tiny red pot. It was delicately made and decorated with a carved motif of roses. She opened it carefully. It contained a smooth reddish-pink paste that smelled of rose petals. Meryall sniffed again and looked at the mixture, not touching the contents of the little pot. It appeared to be a cosmetic but had an odd mineral tang to its scent that she could not identify.

Meryall carried the red container over to Madoc, who examined the contents keenly.

'Aelcea showed me this pot when I connected with her spirit. Do you think it might contain some sort of poison?'

Madoc nodded. 'Please ask Faron and Aelcea's servant when and where she purchased this rouge.' He began taking items from his bag, and filling a small cauldron from his pack with water, he set it to boil at the fireplace. Madoc pounded charcoal, dried seaweed and garlic in his pestle and mortar and poured the powder into a horn cup. He was sitting waiting for the water to boil and observing Aelcea's breathing and pulse as she slept when Meryall came into the room with Faron. He took up the pot and considered it, frowning.

'I believe she must have purchased it only within the last two weeks; I don't often recall her wearing rouge before. I do not know where she found it, however… Do you believe that this is a poison? Will she be well again now you have discovered it?'

Madoc took up the cauldron as it began to steam and poured water into the cup, stirring it vigorously with a wooden spoon. A smell of the sea, combined with the sharp smell of the freshly mashed garlic filled the room. Madoc set it aside to cool.

'If the exposure has not been over a long period, we can help to force the poison from her system. I believe it to be a mineral often found abroad – cinnabar, which is used to make vermilion. The Romans knew it to be poisonous and yet it is still found in cosmetics from time to time. It is dangerous to the body and can cause serious damage to the organs, but I hope that regular doses of this mixture, combined with sweat baths, will help to bring the poison out of her body and restore her to herself. I will oversee her care for a few days more to see how she responds. In the meantime, it would be helpful to find out where she purchased the rouge. I think it advisable to speak to Lord De Lune's people to ascertain whether they know of any stallholders selling cosmetics.'

'Should we send word to Richard?' Meryall asked.

Madoc hesitated. 'Perhaps not today. I would like to see how Aelcea responds to her first treatments,' he replied.

Meryall looked sideways at him, surprised by his reticence to share his discovery with his fellow apothecary, but readily agreed to his suggestion.

Madoc remained with Aelcea and her servant for the

remainder of the afternoon. He diligently administered doses of his mixture, showing her servant how to make it. He supervised the preparation of sweat baths, a basin of boiled water placed carefully under a tent of blankets to make Aelcea sweat heavily, and gave detailed instructions about the disposal of clothing and linens exposed to the poison, excreted through Aelcea's skin as she perspired. The whole household was occupied in caring for Aelcea, eager to follow his orders.

Avarall and Meryall went down to the market to speak to Lord De Lune's men and to search amongst the market stalls. The streets were still busy, despite the afternoon light beginning to darken. They went first to the market office, situated in a square block of administrative buildings to the side of the courtyard. The firelit cosy atmosphere of the room was enhanced by the presence of a comfortably built man in a fur-trimmed robe. His round face shone with good humour, and he rose to his feet with a smile to greet them.

'My good ladies! I am Percy De Lune, Steward of Lune Castle. How may I be of service?' He executed a short bow and stood with an expression of polite interest on his face.

'Sir, we require your assistance in a most important matter,' Meryall began.

'Indeed!' Percy said swiftly. 'Matters of importance require a comfortable seat and a drink.' He indicated a bench before the fire and took cups and a flagon of wine from a sideboard. Percy sat in a high wing-back chair opposite them and poured drinks. He raised his drink in a gesture between a toast and an invitation to proceed.

Meryall sipped her wine, regarding him for a moment before she began. She felt unsure whether to trust the apparent jolly benignity in this man, who after all was the right-hand man of a lord well known for ruthless practices. 'You are a relative of Lord De Lune?' she said.

Percy inclined his head. 'A cousin, yes. And you, I believe, are residing in the household of another of my kinsfolk – Faron Allred.'

Meryall smiled. He had shown his hand quickly, which reassured her somewhat.

'I see that introductions are unnecessary,' she replied.

'Your reputations precede you both,' Percy said smoothly.

'As you will know, we are seeking to treat Mistress Aelcea. We believe that she may have been poisoned by a pot of rouge.' Meryall produced the little pot from the pouch at her waist and held it out to Percy. 'We wanted to consult with you to ascertain whether she purchased the rouge from one of the stallholders. Knowing the origins of the cosmetic may help us to understand the contents – and consequently the best treatment … as well as avoiding further danger to others.'

Percy took the pot in his hand. It sat in the centre of his large, square palm as he examined it carefully. 'I would say that the container was made in the Far East,' he said. 'But such pots are often purchased by merchants to be filled with perfumed balms or cosmetics, which makes the origins of the contents more difficult to trace.' He looked at Meryall sharply. 'And you have come to the conclusion that it was most likely a product of the market?'

Meryall shrugged. 'Your knowledge of the town will tell you whether this is likely to be so – or whether there are other shops where Mistress Aelcea may have procured something of this nature.'

Percy handed back the pot. 'I will have my men make enquiries amongst the merchants, but I cannot recall having seen anything similar when I have been making my rounds.'

'Thank you, your assistance is most appreciated,' Meryall replied.

Percy smiled and bowed. He turned to look at Avarall. 'Your reputation as a tracker and archer is well known to me, Mistress Avarall,' he said. 'If you ever wish to join your relative at Lune Castle, Lord De Lune would welcome someone of your skill to his service.'

Avarall returned his gaze. 'I thank you for the compliment, Master Percy. However, my sheriff has earned my lasting loyalty and service.'

Percy raised his eyebrow and gave a half smile. 'I am sure that his gain is our loss.'

They stood, handing back their wine cups with parting pleasantries. Meryall and Avarall walked in silence for some way from the offices, moving amongst the stalls with the intention of appearing interested in the goods they were selling.

'Master Percy is remarkably well informed,' Avarall said after she judged that they had moved a safe distance from his hearing.

'Indeed – and he was at pains to ensure that we were

aware of his knowledge,' Meryall replied. Their search was fruitless –the stallholders were packing up, and they were unable to locate any stands selling cosmetics.

They returned to the Allreds' quarters. The smell of charcoal and garlic hung in the air, and the servants bustled about, boiling water for steam baths and disposing of sweat-dampened clothes. The misted windows filtered the pink-tinged afternoon light, suffusing the house with a warm blush.

Madoc was still above stairs, so Avarall and Meryall parted to rest until the evening meal, eager not to inconvenience the busy household.

Meryall sat alone in the quarters she shared with Madoc, looking out across the river. She had rarely been away from home for more than a night or so – and even then, only to visit neighbouring villages. She looked with interest at the scene before her, noticing the subtle differences in the stone that formed the buildings of Lune, compared to that of Thornton Cleveleys. The afternoon light shone on fisherfolk returning from their labours and the river barges of merchants. The tousled heads of children caught her eye as they darted between the crowds, hoping to find a fallen fish for their dinner, or racing sticks that they dropped into the fast current. The sounds of the castle and the town around them were a constant background drone here, unlike the deep quiet that filled Horn Cottage, where only the soft sounds of the birds and the wind in the trees penetrated the thick walls.

It was pleasant to sit watching the people below her and Meryall noticed with surprise the fading light, hinting it was already time for their meal. She washed her face and hands, brushed down her dress and went to join Faron and Avarall at the table.

Madoc joined them, sinking gratefully into his seat, rubbing his eyes with the heels of his hands. He smiled, taking Faron's hand.

'She remains fatigued and weak, but her colour is better and her pulse stronger.' Faron's eyes filled with tears at the news and he wrung Madoc's hand, unable to voice his thanks.

Chapter 8

The following morning, in need of air and exercise, they walked about the courtyard for some time, exploring the stalls and searching again for purveyors of cosmetics amongst the merchants. Meryall saw the red-and-gold-cloaked man once again. Avarall, catching the direction of her gaze, whispered that it was Lord De Lune. He had also observed them and approached them, hailing Avarall and giving his regards to the sheriff. Avarall politely bowed her thanks and introduced Meryall and Madoc. Lord De Lune bowed with grace and smiled at them both.

'It is the closing day of the market today, and we are to have a feast – you would do me a great honour if you would attend.'

They accepted his invitation with thanks.

'I wonder, sir,' Meryall asked casually, 'if you could tell me who sells the finest perfumes and cosmetics?'

'Ah, madam, I perceive that your search has met with no success. My cousin Percy informed me of your predicament.

We have been unable to locate any merchant with goods which match the description Percy circulated, to my sorrow.'

Meryall thanked him and turned the conversation to the goods on offer on the most elegant stands they had seen. They passed some time in discussing the various baubles they had admired at the stalls. Lord De Lune turned away with a bow, his men following at his heels, as he continued to walk amongst the stalls.

Once back in the hall of the Allreds' quarters, they exchanged glances.

'Well, Meryall, what did your sight tell you of our lord?' Madoc asked.

'I do not need the sight to get his measure!' Meryall laughed. 'He is a clever man, ruthless and able to charm where he wishes to … and yet his presence creates an uneasiness in people that means that others often distrust him. What do we know of his family and early life?'

Avarall considered for a moment. 'His father was known to be a skilled warrior and hunter. He was well respected, but not well liked. He was said to be a difficult man within his home, severe with his children and quick-handed with his wife. He died after a hunting accident shortly after Lord De Lune came of age. It was a lucky thing that it happened no sooner, as otherwise there would have been no one of age to look after the estate. Lord De Lune's sister married young and moved far from the castle, and his mother died some years before his father. Many of the neighbouring nobles fear Lord De Lune, but people tolerate him because of the prosperity he brings to the town and surrounding areas. I suppose that it is his wolfish ways that make him so good at buying and selling.'

'And he has not married or settled?' Madoc asked.

'No,' Avarall replied. 'There was some talk about him marrying a rich merchant's daughter, in the hopes of creating strong trade links with her family … however nothing came of that. He is rumoured to have a glad eye though and is known to take up mistresses and grow disinterested with them often. There are whispers that one woman was not happy to be cast aside and threatened to expose Lord De Lune to the merchant's daughter he intended to marry. He made her a settlement, buying her a house some distance from the village.'

'You have been diligent in collecting information about Lord De Lune, Avarall,' Meryall said. She appreciated Avarall's thoroughness. It was a skill to pull details from many sources and present them coherently. The sheriff's forces were well known for the thoroughness of their training and Wyot, though kind and patient, was an exacting master, who expected – and received – the highest standards from his people.

'We are no further forward in finding the origin of the rouge,' Avarall said.

'Well, if we cannot find it amongst the merchants,' Madoc said, 'there will be few people in town who have access to items such as cinnabar and vermilion other than the apothecary. However, I would like to be assured about his honesty before I speak to him about this, and therefore I think it would be best to wait until we can examine his shop without him being aware.'

They agreed to visit the apothecary shop the next day and parted, Avarall to the stables and Meryall and Madoc to take a walk along the banks of the River Lune.

Avarall had frowned at this initially, keen to accompany them, but was eventually persuaded of the safety of the open pathway and the bright daylight.

Meryall was pleased to be alone with Madoc for a little while. The business of the investigation had not allowed them time to enjoy the rare experience of being away from home together. The grave purpose of their trip was never far from her mind, but she felt the small thrill of a schoolchild given a half-day holiday at the prospect of a free afternoon with Madoc in an unfamiliar place.

Meryall walked with a light step and Madoc, observing her flush of pleasure, squeezed his arm about her waist. The road soon took them out of the town and down to the river banks. Still and sluggish near the town, as they walked on, the River Lune sparkled in the sun as it gained pace to rush over its stony bed. They savoured the fresh scent of the clean water in the air – the close, potent smells of the town were soon forgotten, carried away by the breeze. Meryall heard Madoc's stomach growl. She wished she had thought to ask Faron for supplies – they could have sat beneath a tree and eaten a pleasant meal beside the water.

'Should we turn back? I recollect that we have not eaten since breakfast and it is now well past noon!'

Madoc shook his head. He indicated a large, flat stone a

little way off the path, near the river, and opened his leather satchel to show a flask, bread and other packages.

'I believe that you will find quite enough for us to feast upon in here.'

Meryall was delighted. 'When did you pack a meal for us? What a wonderful surprise!'

Madoc's eyes crinkled in satisfaction at the effect of his artful plan. 'When you went to change your shoes and to put on a cloak, I asked Faron's servant to pack up my satchel quickly for us and return it to me closed, with my cloak, so that you would not notice.'

Meryall laughed. 'A very smooth and pleasing deception. I was beginning to wish I had thought to pack a meal for us to eat.'

'I had been waiting for you to say that you were hungry – but my stomach grew impatient and forced the issue.'

The troubles of Lune, the Allreds, Avery and Eda felt far away as they sat on the cool, dry stone, unpacking cloth-wrapped bundles. The satchel yielded a piece of rich, sharp cheese, two apples, a stout pie filled with pork, and a flask of ale. The day was cool, but they were warmed by their walk, and the sun caught their backs and lent them its heat as they sat, chatting about their businesses, neighbours, plants and hopes for the spring to come.

'Do you ever think of travelling overseas again?' Meryall asked Madoc.

He settled himself on the stone and looked into her face for a long moment before replying. 'I relished my journeys and am grateful for the knowledge I gained on my travels,' he said carefully, 'but I will not leave Albion again unless you come with me.'

Meryall focused her attention on the ground. An ant made tiny journeys to and fro at her feet, intent on some unknown task. Meryall flicked a crumb towards the ant and waited to see if he would locate it. The ant continued his miniature military fatigues, following his unknowable little regime amongst the blades of grass. Meryall, lost in thought, started when Madoc placed his hand on her arm.

'Do you feel discontent in your life?' he asked her, his voice gentle and earnest, his face shadowed with sadness.

Meryall shook her head, attempting to answer with liveliness, to cheer Madoc and chase the melancholy from their bright afternoon. 'No, indeed, I have much to be thankful for. It is just that the weight of responsibility for the village fell on me early and allowed little time for my own interests and concerns.'

'Well,' Madoc said thoughtfully, 'your responsibilities are no cage… Master Arledge's apprentice is now of an age where he is fairly advanced in his learning of the cunning ways, yet Arledge is too proud and vigorous to retire from his village just yet. If you choose to take a sabbatical, I am sure that young Turi would happily come and look after Horn Cottage and Thornton for you.'

Meryall looked at him in surprise. This had not occurred to her. Her mood lightened – to be free to leave, without guilt, was a great thing and opened up her horizons considerably. In excellent spirits, they talked on with renewed vigour and a different nuance to their discussions of Madoc's travels – the places he had been and the places he had heard of but had yet to go.

All too soon, the meal was done, and the sun began to move towards late afternoon. It was time to return to Lune, for there was a feast to prepare for. Meryall felt a twinge of sadness that they could not remain wrapped in their own small concerns, interested only in each other a while longer. She chided herself for selfishness. There were many matters of greater importance that they must attend to.

Chapter 9

Back in their quarters, the dust and sweat of the walk washed away, Meryall put on her best dress – a green satin overdress gathered with a gold embroidered belt over a cream cotton chemise. The green set off her dark hair and contrasted with the lighter green tone of her eyes. The gown was cut well – it revealed her shoulders and skimmed her bust, fitted snugly to her waist and then fell in a full skirt.

Fashion was much influenced by trading partners in France and further afield, but Albion was a small country whose territories spread only to the land of the Cornish in the south and the Scots in the north, with the Welsh border soft and permeable – and it had developed its own styles.

The fashions women wore varied widely, dependent on occupation, means and inclination. Meryall wore breeches on some occasions, but enjoyed the swirl and movement of a skirt, particularly if she was attending a feast, where she felt elegant in her sweeping dress. She added a necklace of delicately wrought silver ivy leaves, symbolic of her rank as a cunning woman, fastened close to her neck. Meryall arranged her dark hair in a mass of plaits and regarded herself with satisfaction in the mirror.

Madoc had dressed in a linen shirt and blue doublet, with gold detailing along the hems with matching breeches, and had gone down to sit for a while with Faron, who did not wish to leave Aelcea to come to the feast.

'Come in!' Meryall called, in reply to the soft knock on her door.

Avarall stepped in, dressed in a fine crimson dress uniform, with a high collar and tall buckled boots.

She had twisted her hair into a crown of golden braids, threaded with red ribbon.

The style suited Avarall – revealing her strongly drawn cheekbones and bright blue, almond-shaped eyes.

'You look magnificent!' Meryall said, walking around Avarall to admire her attire.

'I was just coming to check that you thought this was appropriate for the feast,' Avarall replied, smiling.

'Yes, indeed,' Meryall said, 'you look most arresting.'

They walked downstairs together, finding Faron and Madoc sharing a jug of mead before the fire. They took a small cup to toast the health of all present – and especially to ask for blessings from the gods and goddesses for Aelcea, then bade Faron farewell and set out for the castle's great hall.

The evening was cool as they walked through the deeply shadowed courtyard. Torches sat in brackets along the walls to light the way for the many guests, but the night sky was heavy and overcast, with few stars or moonlight to relieve the gloom. Meryall looked at the people around her – men and women in fine gowns, picking their way through the pools of dark ground, fearful of befouling their shoes in the mud, horse droppings and occasional suspicious sodden sections of earth near the doorways and alleys.

The light from inside dazzled them. Dozens of candles lit the hall, suspended in many-armed candelabras hung above the long table. Tapestries woven with the De Lune crest of a crescent moon upon a blue ground, wreathed with decorative borders of hares chasing through the golden corn, to symbolise the prosperity and wisdom of his house, hung from the walls, adding warmth and colour to the hall. Guests were milling about by the fireplaces at either end of the room, exchanging news and market gossip. Many people were dressed in garments made of cloth that Meryall recognised from the stands – expensive brocades imported from Constantinople, velvets from Genoa and tightly woven, bright woollen cloth from Bruges.

A burst of notes from the herald's bugle invited them to take their places. They found a pair of seats, with a third opposite, halfway down the table. Avarall and Meryall sat side by side, with Madoc facing them across the broad table. Meryall's neighbour was a sharp-faced slender old woman, who sat turned half away from her, talking to an elderly man she took to be her husband or lover. Avarall found herself quickly engaged in conversation with a fine-looking soldier, who asked her many questions about her rank and experience and listened intently, stealing admiring glances at her profile whenever she addressed her fellow diners. Madoc was flanked by two gregarious Flemish merchants, who had made a good profit on their cloth and were eager to celebrate their successes with feasting and merrymaking. They made amorous enquiries of Madoc about the rites of spring and of the rights of women to lie with whom they chose within or without wedlock. Madoc concluded that these civilised matters were entirely foreign to their culture.

A further sounding of the trumpet silenced the guests. Lord De Lune stood at the head of the table, a cup raised in a toast. 'My dear friends, let me open our feast with this blessing … may your cups be full, your cullions be emptied and your heart content!' There was a raucous roar of laughter and cheering, followed by much foot stamping and the emptying and raising of cups to be refilled. Meryall had rolled her eyes at the crudeness of the toast and Madoc was occupied in explaining the meaning of 'cullions' to the Flemings, who eventually understood and laughed until tears filled their eyes, slapping Madoc's shoulders in the excess of their mirth. Meryall sighed. The Flemish merchants were typical of a particular type of man who travelled to Albion, filled with tales of the wild sexual appetites of the godless women there. Often, they were pious and restrictive of their wives and daughters in their Christian homeland, but more than willing to seek the company of women with sexual freedom and independence in another land.

Serving men and women moved around the tables, bringing enormous dishes of roast venison, platters of cheeses, and loaves of bread, fruits and river fish freshly caught and cooked with sharp sorrel leaves and garlic. The group ate well, drinking cups of rich, dark French wine and talking with animation to their fellow guests. There were many languages spoken around the table – and their English hosts understood the merchants well. The excellent trade connections that Albion had developed around the world and the superb quality of its universities had combined to create a population extraordinarily conversant in many languages. Even the common folk had some knowledge of French and Latin. Knowledge of Greek, German and Spanish was not at all unusual, in addition to fluency in the languages of the Celtic peoples.

The elderly couple, who had remained cheerless and sober throughout the dinner, left the table, nodding a farewell in the direction of their host as they walked out towards the courtyard. A young man sat down next to Meryall. She took him to be no more than twenty-one years old. He wore a Roman Christian's tonsure and robe, but his merry eyes and ready smile were at odds with the markers of his austere vocation.

'I hope you don't mind me joining you, mistress, but my previous neighbours have become wearisome.' He gestured towards a group of Italian merchants further up the table, who had begun to argue heatedly over their cups of wine. Meryall smiled in sympathy. The Flemish merchants continued to monopolise Madoc's conversation, and Avarall and her handsome neighbour were engaged in an intense tête-à-tête, their surroundings apparently fading from their awareness. She was glad of some pleasing company.

'You are Italian, I think.'

The young man inclined his head. 'You are quite right, mistress. I am Brother Florian – I am on a journey to the great University of York. My order in Rome has sent some of its scholars to study the skies there, for your knowledge is reputed to be exceptionally advanced.'

'You are taking a long route to York, Brother! How came you to be in Lune?'

Florian laughed. 'You are most astute – I have found the British people to be so fascinating that I confess my journey has been unnecessarily lengthened!'

Meryall joined him in laughter. 'I am not sure what your order will make of your interest. I know that the Roman Church considers us to be a heathen, godless people.'

'Indeed, you are correct. However, the advanced knowledge of the universities and the lucrative trades that the British have in Europe and beyond mean that the Vatican is willing to overlook the sinful nature of its population.' Florian leaned confidingly towards Meryall. 'We are given pamphlets cautioning us on the temptations that we will encounter here – of the wanton womanhood and the bacchanals we may be unfortunate enough to witness.'

Meryall smiled. 'I imagine that has quite the opposite of the desired effect on the young brothers who journey here.'

'Quite so, madam – and so here I am!' Florian raised his cup to Meryall. 'And long may the people of this place continue as they are!' he toasted.

Meryall joined him in the blessing. She paused for a moment after the toast.

'Do you think that the agreement of non-interference that the Roman Church currently has is likely to last? As you know, there have been previous attempts to Christianise us, some of which have been bloody and violent.'

Florian shrugged. 'Access to the trade routes your country controls and the knowledge of your educational institutions is too valuable for the Church to wish to compromise the relationship with Albion.'

'If we were invaded and subdued by a Christian country, the trade routes and universities would be under the control of a ruling power that the Roman Church could benefit from still more than it does now. It would take only the subtle manipulation of a fanatically religious monarch in one of the European nations for our delicate agreements to be threatened,' Meryall said earnestly.

'There is that possibility,' Florian acknowledged. 'However, I believe that there are enough men of sense in positions of authority within the Church to ensure that this does not happen. Albion remains the only pocket of land which is godless in the region– '

'Not godless,' Meryall interrupted. 'We have our own gods, even if we do not believe in yours.'

'Apologies, mistress, I meant no offence.'

Meryall smiled reassurance. 'I took none, but merely wished to clarify that we have our own deities to care for and watch over us.'

'I have no difficulty with this,' Florian said. 'But as you say, there are some who feel that your people should be "saved" from their ways. It is my belief that the importance of your country's standing as a centre of education and commerce protects them from interference, at present.'

'And long may it continue!' Meryall said, echoing Florian's toast and raising her own cup. 'We have been overserious for too long, given the fine meal and wine we have had. Tell me about your travels in Albion so far.'

Florian recounted his landing on the coast and his journey to the small towns and villages he had met along the way.

'We make our home in the village of Thornton Cleveleys, should you wish to visit us on the route back, which I am sure will be equally winding!' Meryall said.

'Ah, Thornton Cleveleys!' Florian cried. 'I know it – I spent a night there and received exceptional hospitality from the sheriff of that place.'

'I would have expected nothing else,' Meryall said with a smile. 'Wyot is a great man and a fine sheriff. I am the cunning woman of the village – if you have encountered the term?'

'Yes, I understand that cunning folk are the people who practise magic – throw off the evil eye or make love charms and such things.' He gave a wry laugh. 'There is a whole page devoted to cunning folk and witches and their blasphemous ways in that pamphlet I mentioned.'

Meryall threw back her head and laughed. 'And am I as you feared?' she enquired.

'No, mistress, you are as I hoped,' Florian said, with a small bow and a wink.

The hour was growing late; Meryall caught Madoc's eye

and stood to go. Avarall immediately stood, ready to escort them, an apologetic smile to her soldier companion. Meryall suspected that she would rejoin him after seeing them home and smiled at the young woman, whose flushed cheeks and bright eyes showed her lively interest in her new acquaintance. Introducing Florian to her companions, Meryall took her leave. Her invitation to Florian to visit them if it happened to be on his way home was warmly seconded by Madoc and Avarall.

As they passed through the hall, Meryall noticed that Lord De Lune's chair at the head of the table was empty.

'We will have to pay our respects to our host tomorrow,' she said, grateful not to have to delay their exit with ceremonious farewells.

The night was cool as they crossed the courtyard towards the Allreds' quarters. Avarall placed a strong hand on Meryall's arm, halting her step. She placed her finger to her lips – they listened. A gasping sound reached their ears, followed by a soft thump. Avarall ran swiftly towards the sounds, Madoc and Meryall at her heels. In a shadowed niche of the stone walls, Avarall saw a cloaked figure and grabbed its shoulder, spinning the man around.

'Oh! Apologies, sir!' Avarall's cheeks crimsoned – Lord De Lune stood before her, breeches unbuttoned and face filled with annoyance. A bright, female laugh rang out. A young woman, dress hitched to her thighs, covered her face and giggled, pushing her skirts down with her other hand.

'Indeed, my honoured guests, you find me attempting to fulfil the latter part of my own blessing!' De Lune said smoothly, not troubling to close his breeches, but swirling his cloak elegantly to cover himself. 'You must forgive the neglect of my duties as a host. However, I have other duties to attend to…' He turned back to his partner, arm slipping around her waist, triggering further giggling from the young woman in his grasp. They wished him many blessings, departing with as much dignity as they could muster.

In Faron's lounge, they sat in a thoughtful silence awaiting their mulled wine.

'Well, Lord De Lune's reputation with women is well earned,' Madoc said.

'Indeed.' Meryall looked thoughtful. 'His partner appeared content in his attentions. I wonder if Eda was also charmed by Lord De Lune.'

'But if she were, it is no problem – as long as she and he were willing – it is no reason to run away – or to be taken away by force,' Avarall added.

'I can well imagine a broken heart or bruised pride as reason enough to run away – Lord De Lune is evidently generous in the bestowal of his affections … but what reason, other than villainy, could there be for him to wish her harm, even if he had grown tired of her?' Madoc said.

'I think that tomorrow we must find a way of speaking to the staff of his household,' Meryall suggested. 'But now, mulled wine and sweet dreams are our primary concern, I feel.'

Avarall looked self-conscious. 'By your leave, I would pay a visit to a friend for an hour or two.'

'Of course!' Meryall and Madoc said together, hiding their smiles in their cups.

Avarall threw on her cloak and bidding them blessings for a peaceful night, stepped smartly down the stairs.

'And so, to bed for us, too?' Meryall asked, smiling at Madoc, who laughed as he swept Meryall from her feet, kissing her lips as he lifted her, arm around his neck, to the stairs. Giggling, they shushed themselves as Madoc caught Meryall's feet on the panelling with a thud as he carried her along the corridor to their room.

Chapter 10

The courtyard of the castle was quiet the next morning – the excesses of the night before had kept many who had the luxury of remaining in their beds there, and those merchants who had not that option made their departures sore of head and delicate of stomach. Avarall suppressed a smile. She did not envy those wealthy merchants their swaying waggon, river and sea voyages, in the midst of their thick heads and queasiness.

Avarall walked through the archway to the servants' quarters, a recipe in her hand written by Madoc as her excuse for her presence there. Madoc had requested some arrowroot for Aelcea, having apparently neglected to pack any in his medicine bag. She passed the apothecary on the stairs and waved to him, hoping that he did not stop to speak to her and do away with her excuse by offering assistance of his own. However, he merely turned his head to watch her pass.

The passages were swept clean, and there was the smell of clean linen and fresh bread in the air. The servants' quarters and kitchens appeared to run efficiently. Avarall had an elderly cousin who lived in the servants' quarters serving a nominal role as a dressmaker, and so she turned towards the stairs and proceeded up to the rambling attics which served as stores and sleeping quarters.

She walked through a long dormitory which she guessed, from the articles of female attire strewn over the furniture, was the area reserved for the maids. Ensuring that she was not observed, she began to make an inspection of the room. The floor had recently been swept and patted down afresh, making it impossible to trace the scraped floor that Avery Greenhalgh had spoken of in his meeting with Meryall. Avarall was about to look under the beds when she heard a step in the corridor.

Straightening hastily, she moved towards the door and called out, 'Ho there! I wonder if you can tell me where I may find Mistress Rose?'

A plump woman stepped forward and eyed Avarall suspiciously. 'And what is your business here that you wish to know this?'

Avarall smiled and lowered her eyes. 'Mistress Rose is my cousin. I was asked to visit the kitchens to seek some arrowroot for the Allred household but wished to use the occasion to pay my respects to the good lady. I remember her fondly, but rarely have the opportunity to see her.'

The woman softened. 'Indeed, Mistress Rose is a kind, sweet woman. I do not wonder she is valued by her family. She has many visitors. I am Ursula, head of the servants here. I will show you to her quarters and bring you refreshments. Did you say it was arrowroot you need?'

Avarall nodded. 'My companions are treating Mistress Aelcea but did not have arrowroot available to them and had been told that the kitchens here were likely to be well-supplied.'

'You were not misinformed,' Ursula said, with obvious pride. 'Our lord's talents as a merchant mean that the quality and breadth of our stores is remarkable. You will find some fine arrowroot if you pass by the kitchen after your visit.'

They walked through the dormitory and on up a further flight of stairs.

'Your cousin will tell you that in addition to our stores of rare spices, wines and other delicacies, the linens belonging to our household are very fine – even the clothing of the servants is made of beautifully woven cloth, soft and skilfully dyed.'

'Ah! Then I do not doubt that you have little trouble in keeping staff here,' Avarall said casually.

Ursula glanced over her shoulder. 'Less than other large households, I should expect.'

They reached the door of a round chamber, flooded with light from five tall windows and cosily furnished with tapestries, seats and a bed. A woman, old but graceful, stood as they entered. 'Avarall!' she said, coming forward to kiss her cousin's cheeks.

'It is good to see you, Rose,' Avarall replied, squeezing Rose's hand.

'I will bring you some refreshments,' Ursula said, closing the door with a warm smile.

'You are comfortable here, Rose?' Avarall asked.

'Indeed, child. I am well-looked-after. I work only a small amount – I am still able to make detailed work and embellish the garments of Lord De Lune himself, as well as supervising and instructing some of the young women in needlework. In return, I have the use of this chamber, plentiful food and drink and am promised a pension when I am no longer able to work.'

'Lord De Lune is a generous employer,' Avarall said, taking a seat next to Rose on a low wooden bench covered with cushions decorated with Rose's fanciful designs of horned figures, oak leaves and animals.

'And how do you find your work for the sheriff?' Rose asked.

'I find him to be exacting of himself and others, but generous and honest. He is a man of integrity.'

'I am pleased to hear it, child. It is of great importance, especially for a young woman, to be safe and well respected by her employer.' Rose looked serious for a moment. Avarall was about to press her further when Ursula's step rang on the stairs. She entered the room, skilfully opening the door with one hand while balancing a tray in her other. Ursula placed down a pitcher of fresh, foamy milk, which was softly scented with cinnamon and flavoured with honey; seed cakes; a warm loaf of bread and a soft, creamy goat's cheese.

They thanked Ursula and she withdrew, leaving them to talk, eat and drink in peace. For an elderly woman, Rose retained a lively appetite. Avarall observed this with a laugh, hoping that her own good appetite would continue to be strong.

'I wanted to ask you if you knew a young woman by the name of Eda Greenhalgh who was a servant in this household,' Avarall said after they had finished their meal. Rose looked at her for a long moment.

'I had wondered why the sheriff had sent you and his friends to aid Aelcea … there are many fine apothecaries and cunning men and women hereabouts who may have offered a second opinion where Richard had found his medicines to fail. He takes an interest in Eda's disappearance, does he?'

Avarall smiled at her cousin's perceptive mind. 'Indeed, Rose. Her brother feared that harm had come to her – and it appears that harm came to him when he sought to find out more.'

'Well, I cannot say that Lord De Lune is as honest as your sheriff … indeed, their different lines of work mean that it is unlikely to be otherwise. A cunning merchant is a rich one, but an underhand sheriff is a poor servant to his people. However, I would think it unlikely that Lord De Lune would have caused Eda any harm. I knew the girl a little; she came to me to learn needlework. She was a very pretty girl – with great dark eyes, thick hair curling to her waist and a sweet figure. She was clever and kind, but an ambitious girl. I had a sense that she did not intend to remain a servant but had an eye to the main chance.'

'And who could blame her, cousin? Every man is the maker of his own fortune,' Avarall replied, thoughtfully.

Avarall made her way through the passageways and down the stairs until she found herself in the kitchen. A sturdy cook was turning a joint of meat in a large fireplace at one end, his forearms beaded with sweat from the effort and the harsh heat of the fire.

'Are you the head cook, sir?' Avarall called out.

The man turned towards her and frowned, not recognising her face. 'Can I help you, mistress?'

'Ursula said that I might come and borrow some arrowroot for the Allred household,' Avarall explained.

'Ah! She said that a young woman would stop by for arrowroot. You are cousin to Mistress Rose?'

'Yes – it has been a pleasure to visit her today and to find her well-looked-after.' Avarall watched the big man moving nimbly about the kitchen stores, taking out a jar and filling a small box with powdered arrowroot.

'I was sad to hear of the death of one of the servants from this house,' she said.

The cook continued to work, his back to her, but Avarall was sure that she had seen him tense at her words.

'You are better informed than I am, mistress.' He continued to move around, putting things back in their place, before turning to face her.

'Well … not a servant of this house exactly, but rather the brother of Eda, who sought to find her, has been found dead in suspicious circumstances. It makes me wonder if Eda is not dead also.'

The cook looked at Avarall for a long moment, seeming to search for words. 'I would be surprised if that was so. Eda was a strong-minded young woman, kind-natured and sweet-tempered, but determined to make her own way and sharp. I cannot see her getting into a situation where she might be in danger.'

'Your Lord De Lune has a reputation with women, I believe.' Avarall knew this was a risky line of questioning but judged the cook to be placid and unlikely to report her inquisitiveness. The cook looked amused.

'Indeed, he is overfond of female company. However, he treats his women well … lately, he has taken it into his head to try to marry one of the German merchant's daughters, to secure trade links with him. He knows that, although we do not care at all about whether people are wed or no if they like to be with one another, the Germans do. He has been rather careful of late that any children of his and any former lovers who are less likely to be trusted to be discreet have relocated to other villages … with a fine package of compensation for doing so.'

'How do you know this?' said Avarall, astonished that this piece of information had not reached her before, despite her investigations.

'Well, it is not common knowledge amongst the household, however, working in the stores, I have been involved, along with Mistress Ursula, in making up packages of household linen and spices to set up the households of these ladies. I judge it politic to tell you this, mistress, so that you do not go away with the wrong idea about Lord De Lune.'

'And was Eda one of the women who had a household set up for her?' Avarall pressed.

'That I would not know – we were never told who the packages were going to.'

'And the most recent household you set up?'

The cook paused, searching his memory. 'About 10 days ago, I would think.'

Chapter 11

'I am unsure of what to make of this information,' Meryall said when Avarall told them of her visit to the servants' quarters.

'Do you believe that Eda left freely, then, in return for an establishment of her own elsewhere?' Madoc asked.

'Well, either that is so, or people within the household would very much like us to believe it is so.'

'It leaves us with a conundrum – either Eda is living somewhere – in which case, why was her brother killed? Or, she has been killed or taken captive, and we are no further forward in ascertaining where she is, living or dead,' Avarall replied.

'Well, when all earthly methods have failed, perhaps other means are needed,' Meryall said. 'Tonight, I will pay Lord De Lune a dream visit, and we will see if that means of interrogation yields any answers.'

They took heart from this plan and had assembled in the hall for the midday meal when Faron entered the room, looking flushed.

'She is awake and speaking, please, come and see her!' Faron impatiently led them to Aelcea's chambers. Inside, the sun shone through the curtains of her bed, and Aelcea sat, supported by many pillows, still with a tired, drawn face, but lucid, alert and with a little colour to her lips. Madoc smiled and introduced himself and Meryall, seating himself on the edge of the bed to feel Aelcea's pulse, examine the colour inside her eyelids and look into her eyes.

'I remember you both, though I was scarcely able to speak when I saw you last,' Aelcea said.

'We have one or two important questions for you, Aelcea, before we leave you to your rest,' Meryall said, taking up the little red pot and holding it up for Aelcea to see. 'When and where did you purchase this rouge?'

Aelcea thought for a moment. 'I do believe that I bought it from the apothecary shop. It is difficult to say when, I have so confused a sense of how many days have passed since I became ill, but it was perhaps a day or two before we attended a feast with Lord De Lune. Do you remember, Faron?' she said, looking at her husband.

'Yes, it must be around ten days or a fortnight ago,' Faron said.

Aelcea's eyes were wide. 'Richard invited me into the shop as I passed to show me some new wares he had taken delivery of – I purchased some spices and the rouge from him. He was insistent that I purchase it to wear for the feast.'

Faron looked fearful as he considered Aelcea's words. 'Do you think that Master Richard meant Aelcea harm?' he demanded, turning to Meryall and Madoc.

'That is difficult to say,' Meryall replied, 'but I believe we must visit the apothecary's shop once more.'

Fearing that distress might cause Aelcea to lose ground in her recovery, Madoc sat with her for a long time, to calm her with kind words and tisanes. He made up a package of medicine for later on and prescribed a simple, wholesome meal, followed by much rest.

It was late when they finally sat down together to eat. Avarall ate well, as she was wont to do, but Faron sat with his food almost untouched, eyes fixed on his plate. Meryall, aware that she would need strength for her planned night's work, ate nourishing meats, cheeses and fruit and drank a cup of crushed apple juice. Madoc sat absently tracing a pattern on the table with his fingers. Meryall looked at him with sympathy – she knew that he had a delicate sense of professional ethics and honour and that to accuse a fellow practitioner of an action such as this was a serious matter.

An apothecary's duty was to heal, sustain and support life, not to damage it. That was a most heinous crime, a breach of oath, whether the harm caused was intentional or through a lack of care and thoroughness in one's work.

In their room, as they prepared to visit the apothecary shop, Meryall sensed a heavy sadness in Madoc. She took his hand and pulled him down to sit with her on the bed. 'Talk to me.'

Madoc looked down at his feet. 'Would you mind if I went alone, Meryall? I feel that I owe Richard that respect.'

Meryall squeezed his hand. 'No, Avarall and I will leave you to your visit. Come back and tell us what you learn –

just be careful. Richard may not be all that we thought he is … although of course, it may have been a genuine mistake.'

'What motive could he have for wishing to hurt Aelcea? I can only see negligence or ignorance as the root of this issue.'

Madoc's voice carried more conviction than he was able to feel.

Avarall had reluctantly agreed to stay behind, worried for Madoc's safety without her sword at his side.

Madoc stepped out into the courtyard, glad to be alone with his thoughts. The sky was dull and overcast, the air still and sluggish, leaving the smells of the streets to hang in oppressive drifts around him as he walked to the shop, rehearsing what he would say to Richard as he went.

He pictured to himself the possible outcomes of his discussion with the apothecary – would there be an angry confrontation, or would Richard be shocked at his error, contrite, tearful and eager to hear about Aelcea's recovery?

As Madoc approached the shop, he frowned. The shutters were tightly barred. Madoc peered through the joins in the wood. The windows were empty of their stock and the door securely bolted. The apothecary had gone.

Anger surged through the pit of Madoc's stomach. He clenched his hands in his pockets and took a deep breath, letting it out with a whistling sound, before turning back towards the Allreds' quarters.

Avarall stepped out of the shadows of a shop doorway.

Madoc started, then shook his head, laughing.

'I should have known you would come. It was unfair to ask you not to follow me when Wyot had ordered you to stay with us outside of our quarters.'

Avarall bowed her head. 'I apologise, but I did not trust that apothecary.'

Madoc sighed. 'Well, it seems your instincts were good, Avarall. As you see, he is gone.'

They walked back together, their thoughts hanging in the air between them.

The apothecary's disappearance met with a variety of responses. Faron and Aelcea were angry at his perceived desertion following an incident of negligence. Meryall and Avarall were surprised and threw about surmises – had he been forced to leave because of Aelcea's illness and his potential part in it, or was he connected to some other misdeed in the town? Or even, had he been forced to leave? Perhaps Aelcea was not the only person affected, and he had been chased out of town by someone else? Their many questions moved them no further forward, however.

'Well,' Meryall decided, 'it appears that I will need to seek answers to some additional questions during my dream walk. I may be tired and in need of a fortifying breakfast tomorrow.'

Faron promised that they would sit down to a good breakfast in the morning – to allow Meryall to regain her strength and to hear of her adventures.

Madoc took a bed in another room that night to give Meryall the peace and space she required.

Meryall gathered the things she would need before her. She scattered a circle of ash and salt around her bed and laid a garland of herbs around her – mugwort, lavender and dried hawthorn berries. She crushed more of these herbs and made a tisane, drinking down the hot, strongly flavoured liquid. The hawthorn berries had a sweet-sour apple-like taste, which eased the bitterness of the mugwort and complemented the perfume of the lavender.

Placing the cup on the nightstand, Meryall took up a long red thread. She secured one end to the bedpost and the other end to her right wrist. She lay down and closed her eyes. The power of the herbs washed over her in waves as she focused on stepping into a place that was sacred and known only to her – a cave, rather like her own house, but untouched, ancient paintings and stalactites intact in the dark interior, lit by a smoky peat fire.

Meryall sat in front of the fire for a moment, feeling the welcome that she always felt when she came to this place. She stood and reached into the back of the cave, pulling a fox-fur cape from the shadows. The fox's head formed the point of the hood and sat on her forehead. The spirit of the fox would guide her steps, keeping her quiet and agile and allowing her to be sly and mercurial if she had need to be.

Meryall took a stick from beneath her cape and drew the outline of a man on the earth, spitting into the head of the man to form a red hued mud. She pressed her finger into the damp ground, applying a dab of mud to a point between her eyebrows, above the bridge of her nose.

Outside the cave, the woods were cool and still. Three paths curved away into the darkness. Meryall lit a pine knot torch and held the stick she had drawn with before her.

She threw it high into the air. It landed, pointing to the left path. Meryall picked up the stick, tucking it into her belt, and set out along the path.

Amongst the trees, it was dark and the calm night allowed the many small sounds of the forest to reach Meryall's ears. She walked on, the torchlight illuminating the path at her feet, but throwing flickering shafts of light amongst the trees that made the knotted forms of the yew and oak trees appear filled with sinewy limbs and curious faces.

Reaching a crossroads, Meryall stood and waited. At the fork of the path ahead of her, Meryall saw through a gap in the trees a glimpse of a full moon. She continued along the way, watching for a sign that she had reached her destination.

To the side of the path was a great oak tree. The vast trunk was fitted with a rough-hewn door. Meryall took out her stick and rapped on the door three times. The little door swung open, allowing her to step through. Finding herself in a snug chamber well-lit by a fire, Meryall hung her torch in a bracket and strode towards the bed.

There, hair tousled and face relaxed in sleep, lay Lord De Lune. Meryall sat on the edge of the bed, drawing back her hood, and leaned forward to whisper into his ear.

Lord De Lune awoke with a start and sat up, looking in

surprise at the woman seated on his bed. His recovered himself quickly, giving a wry smile.

'Mistress Meryall! Indeed, I had not expected the pleasure of your company at this hour … I am a most hospitable man, you will find.'

Meryall suppressed a laugh. 'I beg you, Lord, come hither and embrace me.'

Lord De Lune's smile broadened as he reached out an arm to encircle her waist and pull her to him. His arm swept through her form. Lord De Lune paled, shock on his features.

'What is this? I do not understand!'

Meryall hushed him. 'Quiet, Lord, do not be distressed. It is but a dream. If you look down, you will see your own sleeping form.'

Lord De Lune glanced frantically around – catching sight of his sleeping body still lying down behind him. He gave a strangled yelp.

'No need to worry, you are but a little outside of yourself, a state we all come to in our sleep from time to time.'

Lord De Lune fixed Meryall with a cool glance. 'If that is so, why are you here too?'

'I have come to pay you a visit. I wanted to ask you about Eda.'

Lord De Lune frowned. 'A strange question for a dream vision! Why do you ask about her?'

'Her brother visited me, concerned about her safety.'

Lord De Lune sighed. 'Ah, yes … Eda asked me not to inform him of our arrangement if he asked, saying that she would contact him when things were properly settled. I was not expecting him to hear about Eda's departure before she had told him, so I honoured her wishes.' Meryall sensed the truth of his words – people seldom lied in their dreams.

'And what was the arrangement that you had with Eda?'

Lord De Lune smiled. 'I miss Eda – a fine woman, strong and ambitious. We had a most passionate affair. However, she knew that I wished to marry Merchant Berenberg's daughter, to strengthen my ties with the trade routes he commands. She proposed to me that it may be in my interests to relocate her to another town, with funds to establish a household and business, to ensure that there were no inconvenient reminders in Lune of my fondness for women. Lovemaking outside of marriage is much frowned upon in those papist countries across the seas.'

Meryall looked thoughtful. 'She blackmailed you?'

Lord De Lune laughed loudly. 'No. Indeed, I was most impressed with her bargaining skills! She is not the first who I have agreed to move, in preparation for the arrival of the Berenberg family for the bride price negotiations, but she was the most ruthless in negotiating her deal. I have no doubt that she will do well in her business.'

'She is unharmed, then?'

'Of course, better than unharmed, she is prospering!'

'Then why did she wish to keep this from her brother?'

'Eda said that her brother had become overprotective – possessive almost – since the death of their parents. She wished to tell him when all was settled and she could invite him to her new home. She hoped that seeing her success and comfort would help reconcile him to what he might otherwise have felt to be me taking advantage of his sister.'

Meryall considered the man before her carefully. 'And where might I find Eda, if I wanted to satisfy myself of her safety?'

'Eda's new establishment is in the village of Samlesbury – as neat a house as you will find, and as fine a mistress of any business you will find, too. Had circumstances been otherwise, she would have been a worthy partner and lover… but alas, I cannot do as I please without thought for the future.'

'I would have thought that the lord of a fine castle such as Lune would need to give little thought to finances, in choosing a wife, if he did not wish to.'

'Ah, indeed, Mistress Meryall, that is a pretty way of viewing the world, but my people have made sacrifices of this nature for many generations to build the castle that you see before you today.'

Meryall shook her head, laughing. 'Well, My Lord, I shall leave you to your dreams – I am sure you have many other fine ladies waiting to enliven your slumber.'

'You are welcome to remain, Meryall. I am sure that what you do in a dream cannot be considered infidelity, so you need not blush in meeting your man in the morning.'

Meryall rolled her eyes and stood, pulling up her hood. 'One more question before I go … what do you know of the apothecary of this town?'

De Lune looked at her in surprise. 'Richard Mangnall? We were friends as boys. I rarely see him now, but I retain his services as the apothecary to the castle, and he joins me for a cup of mead from time to time when he is visiting some sick person within the walls.'

'Did you know he had left town – his shop boarded up, and his goods packed away and carried off?'

'Indeed, I did not. It seems most strange – Richard inherited the shop from his father, it is his family home, as well as his business. Where would he have gone?'

Meryall shrugged. 'Well, I was hoping that you may be able to tell me that, sir. Goodbye Lord De Lune, thank you for your honesty, although you will not remember it tomorrow.'

Lord De Lune sank back into his body as Meryall stepped back out of the dream space he inhabited and made her way back to her sacred place, to ready herself to rejoin her own form.

Chapter 12

Meryall woke to the sun seeping through the curtains of her bed. The herb garland around her had been dispersed by her movements as she slept, the smell of the crushed leaves potent in the still air. She lay still, conscious of the sensations of her body – she ached somewhat in the shoulders, and her legs still retained a faint ache from the long rides of recent days.

Her stomach rumbled with hunger, and her mouth was dry and sour. Tiredness consumed her – the activities of the night before had cost her some energy, but she was satisfied with the new leads that her work had provided. Lord De Lune, she thought, would have been unlikely to have been so honest in the waking world, but his sleeping self, freed from caution and fear of word of his women reaching the merchant or his daughter, had been candid. De Lune, Meryall judged, was a narcissist and an opportunist. A charming blaggard rather than a murdering bastard.

She frowned to herself. The apothecary, however, was a different matter. She struggled to understand his character and behaviour. While Lord De Lune had been able to clarify his own role in Eda's disappearance, he had been able to shed little light on the apothecary's disappearance.

Avery's handsome young face rose in her memory, causing her heart to constrict with sadness, as she remembered the last time she had seen him – dark lashes closed for eternity, casting a faint shadow on his unlined cheeks.

If Eda was alive, did she know of her brother's death? And who had killed him? There were still, frustratingly, far more questions than answers.

Meryall washed her face and hands, swilled her mouth with cool, sweet water, cleaned her teeth with a stick of liquorice root and brushed her hair, freeing it from the tangles of an uneasy night. Feeling fresher, she dressed in an undyed linen chemise with a warm grey woollen overgown and pulled on her soft leather boots.

The boots were her favourites. They had been a gift from Madoc, made of tooled Spanish leather by a craftsman Madoc had come to know on a voyage some years ago when he had acted as ship's apothecary. Meryall regarded herself in the mirror. Her face was rather pale, but she looked respectable enough.

She ran her hands down her flanks. Her gown was fastened with a plain leather belt, with a simple pouch attached to it. She poked the toe of her boots out from her skirts. She would ask Madoc if his merchant friend Jura could bring her a belt and pouch in the same style as her boots next time he was passing through Thornton Cleveleys.

Meryall paused – recalling her conversation with Madoc as they had sat next to the river. Perhaps, she thought with satisfaction, she could purchase her own belt, if their half-formed dream of travelling together came to fruition.

Avarall, Faron and Madoc were assembled at the table, chatting affably as they waited, when Meryall joined them for breakfast. She smiled as they paused in their conversation and looked at her with expectant faces.

'May we at least eat and drink a little first?' she said, laughing. 'I am hungry and thirsty after my night's work!'

'Was it a success?' Avarall asked.

Faron placed a mug of frothy milk before Meryall and handed her a basket of fresh oat bread. Meryall drank a long draught of her milk before answering. 'In many respects, I think so,' she said, buttering her bread as she spoke. 'Lord De Lune was most talkative. I believe that we will be able to find Eda, alive and well, easily enough … but he was unable to tell me anything useful about the apothecary, so I am none the wiser. He was surprised that the apothecary had left town. The shop and apartments above are the apothecary's own. Only an urgent need to be gone would make a man leave his property and livelihood behind.'

'Shall we go in search of Eda today?' Avarall asked.

'I think that would be a sensible course of action – Lord De Lune told me that he has set up a household and business for her in Samlesbury,' Meryall replied.

'It is more than a half day's ride from here. We will need

to stay overnight and return the next day once we have completed our business. I will send word to the sheriff about our plans.' Avarall rose from the table. They heard her quick step on the flags as she went in search of a messenger.

'How is Aelcea today?' Meryall asked.

'Much better!' Faron said, his face bright with relief and joy.

'She is sitting up, able to talk and eat more than yesterday, I am most pleased with her progress,' said Madoc.

'Will you join us on our journey, Madoc, or would you prefer to remain here to oversee Aelcea's care?'

'I believe she is well enough – and so well-cared-for by all in this household – that it will be safe for me to leave her to continue with her herb draughts and steam baths for a day or two.'

Meryall reached across and took his hand, squeezing it. 'Well then, Faron, if you will excuse us, we will prepare for our ride.'

Faron bowed his agreement and bid them a safe journey, offering supplies from his kitchen if they wished to carry provisions for a meal as they travelled.

'Thank you kindly, Faron, but it suits our purpose to dine in a tavern. We have information to seek, and there are few places better to seek the gossip of a town than in its taverns!'

The morning was fresh and bright as they set out on the road to Samlesbury. Once they had left behind the narrow streets of the town and turned away from the rapid, broad river which enclosed Lune in the crescent shape that gave the river and place their names, their path took them through pleasant, rolling countryside. The road was fringed along the eastern side by a far-reaching forest, stretching on for as far as the eye could follow. The companions allowed their horses to maintain a brisk pace, for they had a fair distance to cover.

They passed through small villages, with houses built of a butter-coloured stone that captured the warmth of the sun. The village of Dolphinholme, on the banks of the River Wyre, provided a brief stopping place to water the horses and purchase hot buttered oatcakes from an inn on the main street.

Meryall dismounted with deliberateness, each movement making her aware of her sore muscles, and looked about the village. The street was awash with people – it was market day, and there were stalls of all kinds around them. Avarall found places for their horses in the stable yard of the inn and settled them with fresh water and hay to rest for a short while. Meryall's keen eye found a wheeled wooden stand run by a lady with an upright bearing and a high colour to her cheeks. The little barrow brimmed with herbs and carefully folded packages – this was the cunning woman of Dolphinholme, she suspected. Finishing her oatcake, Meryall walked over towards the stall.

A tall, thin man clad all in black collided with her as he hurried past her. Meryall rubbed her shoulder and turned to watch him, surprised at his rudeness. Madoc appeared beside her, frowning at the tall figure.

'I like not his manners,' he said darkly. They watched the man stride onward. He walked directly to the cunning woman's stall. Meryall unconsciously walked after him, a sense of foreboding growing within her.

'You are an instrument of the devil, woman!' the man shouted, his face white and intense. 'Because of your people, this country remains godless! Because of your kind, our people are doomed to burn in hell!'

The man started forward as if to turn over the woman's stall, but restraining hands reached out from the crowd and steered him away. Meryall looked around. There was shock and concern on the faces of the majority of the people around her, she saw. But here and there, she thought, were faces turned towards the man in black with interest and approval.

There was a sickly, bitter flavour to the mood of the crowd that made her feet itch to move away. Madoc had walked towards the cunning woman, and she followed. The woman was calm and seemed unfazed by the encounter.

'There is a group of Christians who have established a community on the fringe of the forest,' she told Madoc. 'We do not censure them for their beliefs, but some of them are unhappy with the lack of interest their faith generates here.'

'I wonder if there are some in the village who would agree with them, however…' Meryall said, turning to introduce herself to the cunning woman, who gave her name as Orlaith.

'I have heard that their numbers grow in some areas.' Madoc said, 'but I cannot believe that they will impact upon our way of life and our beliefs – the Christians have tried for centuries to save us, but we are immune to their promises and their threats.'

Orlaith remained to chat with them for a time – Madoc had recognised her accent as Irish and spoke with enthusiasm about his travels in her home country. Meryall was curious about whether the customs of the cunning folk differed in Ireland. Orlaith told her that they did not vary significantly, but that Ireland was more Christianised than England and that she had left her home in fear for her life.

Avarall had been making a patrol of the area, looking for the man in black, who seemed to have vanished into the crowds without trace. She rejoined them with a shrug, frowning in dissatisfaction. They parted cordially, with good wishes on all sides, but for Meryall, the incident had left a sense of sadness and anxiety that she found difficult to suppress.

The noon bells had rung when the group reached Samlesbury. They were dusty and had a keen thirst, which made the sight of a neat thatched building with a sign proclaiming it to be the Sunn Inn welcome. Avarall took their horses to the stables at the rear, while Madoc and Meryall entered the tavern's main doors.

The Sunn Inn had an air of comfort, set off by a lively fire, scrubbed tables and the smell of fresh bread. An attractive young woman called a cheerful greeting from the bar, motioning them to a table near the fire.

Putting down the tankard she was polishing, she approached the table and chatted easily with them, offering a meal of rabbit stewed with cabbage and root vegetables and mugs of ale.

They gratefully accepted. The inn was quiet, with no other customers in the main room, but Avarall told them that there were three horses already in the stables, suggesting that there were guests in residence.

The stew was full-bodied and well-flavoured with onions and field mustard greens, and the oat bannock served with it was fresh and warm. Meryall made enquiries about the availability of rooms and was pleased to be told that there were two rooms available that night.

She motioned the young woman to join them for a draught of ale.

'You keep an excellent inn; we are most grateful to come upon it when we are in need of a night's accommodation. Has the inn been in your family for a long time?' Meryall asked.

The young woman laughed cheerfully. 'No indeed, madam. I am new to innkeeping. Thank you for the compliment on how I am managing the Sunn; the previous owner would be pleased to hear that I continue to keep a good house.'

Meryall regarded the young woman carefully. Her dark hair had covered her brow as they entered, but she had now tucked it back behind her ear. Meryall could trace a scar – the same scar she had noted in her vision, although she had not been able to recognise the rest of the face from the fleeting glance she had managed to gain.

'We had hoped, while we were in the village, to meet with a young woman who recently moved here, to ensure she has settled well,' Meryall said with a neutral expression.

A guarded look crossed the features of the young innkeeper. 'Indeed. Many people come to a tavern in search of news and gossip,' she replied, rising from the table, with a forced smile. 'However, I am so new here myself that I have little news to impart.'

'Indeed, Eda, I can imagine that to be the case.'

The young woman stiffened and turned back to face them. Avarall and Madoc looked from Meryall to Eda in surprise.

'We mean you no harm, nor have we come to make trouble. Your arrangement with Lord De Lune is no business of ours … however, your brother was concerned about your well-being. Please, sit and talk with us for a while.'

Eda dropped down onto the bench, keeping her eyes fixed on Meryall. 'And may I know your name, madam, given that you already know mine?'

Meryall introduced herself and her companions and then paused, unwilling to give this bright, sharp-eyed young woman the news of her brother's death.

'Please, sit with us, Eda,' she said softly. 'I am afraid I have unwelcome news of your brother Avery. He has been found dead – we believe he was murdered.'

Eda turned pale, the blood draining from her cheeks and lips. Madoc rose hurriedly and walked behind the bar. After searching for a moment, he returned with a bottle of strong spirits and a cup. He poured a measure for her and put it into her hands.

She looked down at the cup without appearing to see it but soon recovered her wits enough to drain it down, her hands only showing the slightest of tremors.

They sat talking together for a long time. Eda was much affected by the news of Avery's death, but remained coherent and asked many questions about the manner of his death.

'Do you have any idea who may have killed him – or why?' Meryall asked her. 'We had thought that Lord De Lune's men might have killed him to prevent him discovering some harm to you, but that seems unlikely now.'

Eda shook her head, sighing. 'My brother was romantic and foolish at times; I had delayed telling him about my arrangement with Lord De Lune because I feared that he would make difficulties for me, feeling that my honour had not been respected. I trusted that when he saw me established with my own house and business, he would be content and would join me. I had sent word two days ago and was expecting a reply or visit from him anytime now.'

Her eyes filled with tears. 'I cannot think who would have killed him – was he set upon by robbers, perhaps?'

'No,' Madoc said. 'Some coins and a cloak pin were found on his person. Although they were not of much value, if the attack on him were motivated by material gain, these would have been removed.'

Eda wiped her eyes. 'I am sure that Lord De Lune is not responsible – it makes no sense. Killing my brother would be likely to enrage me and endanger the agreement we have made. He does nothing without thought to his own interests.'

'What about his men?' Avarall asked.

Eda shook her head. 'His men are well-trained and well paid. They do nothing without his orders.'

After a few moments of silence, Eda excused herself to start the evening meal for her guests and attend to the business of the inn.

'Wait!' Avarall called. 'When we tracked you, we found tracks which looked like there had been a struggle after which a horse went riderless and a large charger carried two…'

Eda looked puzzled for a while, then gave a hollow laugh. 'When we were riding to come and view this place for my approval, I was in a particular condition – I became nauseous and was forced to dismount suddenly, for fear I would vomit. I retched into the bushes for a while but brought nothing up. I was so sickened, however, that I could scarcely keep my seat and consequently, I rode with one of the men-at-arms until we reached the next town and I was able to take some rest and some restorative herbs. One of the men's horses was bigger than the others and well able to carry my extra weight. We then returned briefly to the castle to collect my goods, although we rode in a cart when we came back, which suited me better, to accommodate the chest of household linens and items that Edward – Lord De Lune – had provided me with.'

'Was the chest placed by your bed while you packed?' Meryall asked.

'Yes, after Ursula added the goods that were gifted to me, we packed my own belongings in the dormitory and moved it out to the corridor for the men to collect and put on the cart.'

That accounted for the drag marks on the floor by her bed, thought Meryall. Two women struggling with a chest would push or drag the heavy weight, leaving the scuff marks on the floor that poor Avery had feared were evidence of some violent act against his sister.

They nodded and were silent, each occupied with a host of questions which remained unspoken.

Chapter 13

Avarall went to check on their horses, and Meryall and Madoc decided to take their bags up to the sleeping quarters assigned to them.

They found their chamber to be well kept, with a large mattress stuffed with fresh-smelling straw and worn but well-laundered linen upon a curtained bedstead. A pitcher of clean water stood on the dresser. Meryall and Madoc washed and changed their clothes, before returning to meet Avarall downstairs.

She was not sitting at any of the tables in the inn when they returned. Madoc suggested that she may still be with the horses and walked around the back of the building to the stables. Meryall seated herself at the table by the fire to wait for her companions.

A sudden shout from the direction of the stables brought her to her feet. She ran outside, the cobbles of the street bruising her feet through the thin soles of her boots. In the stables, Madoc was crouched over a form in one of the stalls. Approaching, Meryall saw that it was Avarall, lying still and pale in the straw beside her horse. Madoc looked up at Meryall, concern in his eyes.

'Please help me to take her inside. I believe she has been struck on the head.'

Taking an arm each, Madoc and Meryall raised Avarall and cradled her between them, hands and arms clasped to hold her in a semi-upright position as they carried her into the inn.

Eda had run to the door, hearing the commotion outside. 'Carry her to her room; I will bring water and cloths to clean her wound,' she said, quickly comprehending what had happened.

She called into the back room. A young boy came running. 'Run to the sheriff's office and tell him there has been attack on a guest.'

The boy turned like a young colt and ran down the street, his long, skinny legs propelling him away with much speed but little elegance.

Madoc and Meryall carried Avarall, now beginning to groan and stir in their arms, up the stairs to the bedroom Eda had pointed out for her. Madoc instructed that they lay her on her side and Meryall remained supporting her while Madoc went to fetch his bag of medicines. Eda returned with clean water and cloths, before going below stairs to boil water, at Madoc's request.

Madoc gently cleaned the wound on the back of Avarall's head, wiping away the blood that had flowed down onto her neck and shoulders to check there was no further injury. Her thick, pale hair was stained with blood from a small cut in the scalp. He inspected the area with care, pressing and feeling to assess the extent of the damage.

Meryall waited, holding Avarall's hair back.

Madoc sat back, wiping his fingers on a cloth. 'She will be fine, she will likely have a fierce ache in her head for a day or two and may perhaps be a little dizzy and unfocused – we must keep a close eye on her, but I do not believe that there will be lasting damage.'

Meryall sighed with relief.

'I will go and search the stables – the culprit is likely to be long gone, but they may have left the implement that they attacked her with.'

The stables were occupied by their own three horses, with another two horses in the opposite row of stalls. A final stall was free, but the stable door was unbolted and swung open. Avarall's horse was uneasy, and Meryall stroked and whispered to her until she was calm before beginning her search of the stall. A horse brush lay in the straw – evidently, Avarall had been brushing her horse down when the attacker struck. Meryall made a close search of the stall but found nothing that could have been used as a weapon.

Giving the horse a final pat and a quick brush, to compensate for her interrupted grooming, Meryall bolted the door and inspected the horses in the other stalls. They were sturdy bay ponies used to much travel, strong and placid. There was nothing unusual in their stalls, or in the stalls of the other horses.

Meryall entered the empty stall and looked around. In the far corner, a glint of light caught her eye. Parting the straw, Meryall found a glass vial. It had broken – dropped from a saddlebag, perhaps, as the owner had left. Meryall took a kerchief from her pocket and carefully picked up the fragments. They contained the traces of a sticky liquid, although most of it had leaked onto the floor. She sniffed it gingerly. The syrupy mixture had an odd, harsh, greenish smell that Meryall recognised. Belladonna – Deadly Nightshade.

Meryall tossed the bottle and her kerchief into the pile of straw and deposited the whole heap into a midden pile at the rear of the stable, digging some rubbish over the top. The liquid was poisonous to man and beast; even the touch of it to the skin could be dangerous. She marked the place with a stone. She would need to tell Eda to burn all that the poison had touched. Meryall filled a bucket with water, washed her hands then threw away the remaining water, ensuring it drained away from the horses. Drying her hands on her apron, she went within.

The sheriff – a young man with striking black hair and beard and ruddy cheeks, was speaking to Eda, two men-at-arms discreetly waiting by the front entrance of the inn, awaiting his instructions. Meryall joined them and added her findings to Eda's account. The sheriff introduced himself as Garrett Allen. Meryall noted that the sheriff was attentive and warm in his manner to Eda. Her thoughts returned to the vial in the stables. The assault on Avarall and the presence of a herbal tincture commonly used by apothecaries in tiny doses as a remedy for pain relief, but extremely poisonous at a higher dose pointed to one conclusion –

Richard Mangnall had been here. Meryall held her tongue. She did not want to say anything that would raise questions about Eda's past in front of the young sheriff. She had a right to her privacy. Garrett accepted the invitation to visit Avarall and followed Meryall above stairs.

Avarall was sitting up in bed, with Madoc seated by her side, when Meryall entered the room. She smiled in greeting and pressed the young woman's hand warmly.

'It is good to see you awake, Avarall!'

Avarall grimaced. 'My head aches like I have drunk half a barrel of mead, but I am otherwise well … the apothecary caught me a stout knock on the head.'

'Ah! You saw the man who hit you?' Garrett asked, striding into the room.

Avarall noted the sheriff's crest upon his breast and raised her hand in salute.

'Yes, sir. I caught a glimpse of him as I turned about – he must have entered the stables after me to tend his horse – I heard footsteps and was just standing from brushing down my horse when I felt a blow to my head, and all is darkness after that, until waking here.'

Garrett apologised for the eagerness which had prompted him to ask questions of her without a proper introduction, giving Avarall his name and rapidly entering into discussion with her about the horse she had observed in the stables before the apothecary's departure and her description of the man. They agreed between them that Garrett would send word to Wyot and would set his men to search the roads for signs of Richard. Garrett took leave of them and went to send messengers and gather his men. Waiting for his footsteps to go down the stairs, Meryall told them of her find in the stable. Madoc's face darkened into a scowl.

'No doubt that he meant to do harm – but who was his target, us or Eda?'

'And why?' Avarall added.

'If he arrived here before us, given that his horse was already in the stable, it is more feasible that Eda was the target,' Meryall said, 'as he would have been unlikely to have realised that we had the means of gaining the knowledge of her whereabouts. It seems to me that for some reason, the apothecary is muddle-headedly invested in safeguarding Lord De Lune's reputation.'

'But why?' Madoc said, his face drawn into tight lines. 'Lord De Lune told you that they had been friends in boyhood, but that they were merely casual acquaintances in recent years. That is not a sufficient incentive for all this scheming and evildoing – and what of Aelcea's poisoning? What motive for that?'

Meryall sighed. 'It appears there is much that we do not know. I think our best option is to return to Lune. We can check on Aelcea and ask her if there is anything she can recollect that might help us understand all this and then go back home and share our discoveries with the sheriff. He may be able to make more of it than we can.'

All agreed with this plan, but fatigue and frustration left a bitter taste in their mouths, robbing them of their appetite.

Nonetheless, they took Avarall a tray of bread, barley broth and cheese and a flagon of sweet new milk and went downstairs to eat their meal, curious to see the other guests and to try to glean some further information about the apothecary from Eda.

The other guests had already taken their seats – a man and woman – a couple in their late fifties, Meryall estimated, their manners suggesting that their companionship had been long and contented. She engaged them in conversation, slipping casual questions about the apothecary into the commonplace remarks about the condition of the roads and the weather. They were unable to tell Madoc and Meryall more than that they had seen him when they arrived. The couple eventually took their leave, retiring to their room to rest.

Eda emerged from behind the bar and joined them. 'Did you learn anything helpful about the apothecary?' she asked.

Meryall smiled. 'It appears that you have the sharp eyes and ears that are so useful in your profession.'

Eda inclined her head. 'I gathered that you suspected that it was the apothecary who attacked your companion, but I have been unable to make sense of why.'

'No more have we,' Meryall acknowledged. 'But we have reason to fear that he intended you harm – can you tell us more about what you know of him? Did you recognise him as the apothecary of Lune? Did he give a reason for his visit?'

'I knew him from Lune – Aelcea Allred recommended him to me, and I had used his services a short while ago. I was surprised to see him here, but he told me that he was on his way to visit his kinsfolk in Ulnes Walton.'

Meryall fought to keep her face calm. 'We did not know

that you were known to Mistress Allred.'

'Yes,' Eda replied. 'I had often seen her about the town, and we came to know each other a little. She found me in distress, suffering terribly from morning sickness one day as I was taken ill in the markets. She kindly took me to her home to wash my face, and I confided my condition to her. She recommended me to the care of the apothecary, telling me that she had used his services many times before and had always found his cures reliable. I went to his shop, telling him that Mistress Aelcea had helped me when I became ill and had suggested I visit to seek a remedy for my sickness. He obliged and provided me with these herbs.' Eda's face darkened.

'What is it?' Madoc asked.

'The herbs alleviated the sickness, but I suffered a miscarriage soon after arriving here.'

Madoc was still and silent. 'Do you have any of the herbs left?' he asked, his face neutral and his voice soft.

Meryall looked at him keenly, finding the traces of tension underneath his studied calm. Eda nodded and disappeared into a back room.

She returned carrying a brown parchment package, tied neatly about with string. Madoc untied it and took a pinch of herbs between his fingers, crushing them to release their scent and examining them closely.

'This is a mixture of herbs which will ease sickness, but which also stimulates the womb and ought not to be used early in pregnancy.'

Eda sat down heavily on the bench. 'What have I done

to the man that he would wish me such harm?'

Meryall took her hand. 'That is what we will seek to understand,' she replied.

Chapter 14

Avarall stated that she was well enough to ride in the morning and so they bid Eda goodbye and set off back to the village of Lune. The day was overcast and cold, with distant clouds threatening rain. The grey skies cast the landscape into muted tones and turned the river at their side to a still, slate grey ribbon. Meryall sensed that their horses were uneasy and wondered if the dark skies on the horizon held a storm.

It was a long ride – Madoc set a comfortable walking pace. He had not been happy with the prospect of Avarall riding so soon after her injury and had proposed staying another night at the inn. Avarall had received word from the sheriff that he would raise men to seek the apothecary and ride out to the neighbouring sheriffs to urge them to do likewise. He also asked that she send word to Lord De Lune to apprise him of the events. Avarall was eager to send a boy with a message for Lord De Lune as they passed through the edges of the town and to get back to Thornton Cleveleys to give Wyot her report in person – and join the action.

The miles trundled by at a leisurely rate. Avarall could ill conceal her impatience at their slow pace, but Madoc appeared satisfied that at midday they were still miles from their destination and unlikely to be able to continue further than Lune, obliging them to stay overnight and providing them with an opportunity to deliver their message personally.

They drew up their horses at a pleasant site in a curve of the River Wyre. The banks were fringed with trees, and a fallen oak provided a makeshift bench. Madoc drew the provisions Eda had packed for them from his bag. She had provided them with generous portions. Madoc handed out slices of mutton and used the knife at his belt to carve thick slices from a large piece of hard cheese with a smooth texture and nutty flavour. Meryall tore the bannock loaf into farls and passed them to her companions. A shared flask of ale and an apple each completed their meal. Avarall's appetite had returned and with it her good humour.

The castle bell was striking three when they arrived at Lune, the sound echoing out over a town still lively with activity. The main street was so crowded that they could scarcely make progress through the press of people. The crowd had gathered in a tight circle around a group of figures that Meryall could not make out. As they drew near, Meryall could see that a band of mummers had entered the town. Their hands were blackened with ashes, ready to rub soot into the fireplaces of householders who cast them money.

Meryall thought about home with a sudden pang of guilt for having forgotten to think of it for some hours at least. At Thornton too the mummers would be making their rounds. It was considered to be a potent symbol of luck and fertility for the mummers to visit and blacken your hearth with their hands and the villagers would be gathered by the market square hoping that the mummers would visit their hearth. Katerin, she knew, was praying for a visit. She brushed the images aside for the moment.

The crushing masses made the prospect of passing through the street near impossible, and they agreed to take the back roads to the Allreds' quarters. In doing so, they walked by the apothecary shop, the windows still empty and blank. Meryall looked up at the sign. Under a painting of a flask amongst an arrangement of herbs was the inscription 'established by S. Helm, 1582'. Meryall drew up.

'I was told that Richard Mangnall inherited the shop from his father – perhaps Richard was blessed with his mother's last name, then. That is helpful to know – there may be Helms hereabouts who know more of his plans.'

Faron Allred received them with warmth. 'Aelcea will be most pleased to see you; she is sitting in the parlour. Please, come in!'

'She is up and out of bed?' Madoc said.

'Indeed, Madoc, she would remain in bed no longer and has insisted on coming down for an hour or two.'

Madoc smiled. 'Well, if her will and spirits have returned

so well, I do not doubt that a change of scene will do her good.'

They followed Faron to the parlour. Aelcea was seated on the window seat, a book in hand, as they entered. Though still pale and thinner in the cheeks than Madoc would have liked, she looked lively and well. She rose and came forward to give them each her hand and thanks. Madoc closely examined her pulse and the response of her eyes and declared himself impressed with her improvement. Faron requested refreshments and gave orders for their rooms to be readied, as it was too far into the day for them to reach Thornton by today's light.

'And what news of the apothecary?' he asked when the servant had withdrawn.

'Grave news and yet little news,' Meryall said. 'We found Eda, and it emerged that the apothecary had also been looking for Eda and with no good intent. Thankfully, we believe we disrupted his plans – at the cost of Avarall's head, unfortunately.'

Avarall firmly declared herself not much the worse for the apothecary's efforts.

'We do not know where he fled to, nor can we fully understand what his purpose is in making these attacks on you and Eda. We did find, however, that it may have been the knowledge of Eda's pregnancy that put you at risk, Aelcea.'

Aelcea frowned. 'But why would Richard care about Eda's pregnancy or who knew of it?'

Meryall sighed deeply. 'That I cannot understand. Nor

can I understand why – if it were indeed him – the apothecary would attack Eda's brother. There are more questions than when we set out to seek answers.'

'I think it would be beneficial if we visited Lord De Lune in person to brief him, rather than merely sending him word,' Madoc suggested. 'After all, these acts may be closely linked to his relationships and actions, whether he had knowledge of the apothecary's plans or not.'

'You are right,' Meryall replied. 'I think it unlikely that Lord De Lune is involved in the commissioning of the apothecary's offences, yet he appears to be the centre of this series of events even so.'

'Our sheriff has requested of us that we communicate our intelligence to Lord De Lune – as we are here, it is fitting that we do so in person,' Avarall added. 'I have Wyot's seal, to ensure that he grants us an audience.'

Faron agreed to dispatch a servant to the castle with their request for an audience.

The messenger returned from the castle and announced that Avarall, Meryall and Madoc were to attend the castle and take their evening meal with Lord De Lune and speak of the matter. The afternoon was already fading into evening, and so they retired to their rooms to wash, change clothes and seek a little rest after the day's fatigues.

In their room, Madoc and Meryall pulled off their boots and fell into the chairs, warming themselves at the fire, not really in need of the heat, for it was not a cold day, but heartened by the warmth. The past few days had laid them open to the deepest darkness of the human soul. Meryall reached out and took Madoc's hand, running her fingers over the well-known callouses.

Meryall's role as a cunning woman had given her a good knowledge of mankind. Her work often involved helping people in distress, those who had suffered or those who wished suffering on others. The petty jealousies and squabbles of village life sometimes concealed more sinister thoughts and actions … and yet, as they learned more, Meryall found the unsavoury details of this mystery to be increasingly distasteful.

She reached out with her essence and touched Madoc's presence. It was as solid and peaceful as ever. Perhaps, Meryall considered, his travels had given him an acceptance of the realities of human nature. He seemed at peace with the good and bad within people and the infinite shades between good and evil that coloured the deeds of men and women.

They were shown to a private chamber within Lord De Lune's quarters, rather than the great hall. The walls of Lord De Lune's chamber bristled with hunting trophies – the heads of stags and boar adorned every wall. Despite this, there was a sense of warmth and good cheer. The room was of modest size and appointed with simple, comfortable furniture, with a litter of books and parchments spilling over on a desk in the window. Lord De Lune rose to greet them, showing them to worn, well-padded chairs by the fire. A jug of sweetened and spiced wine stood warming on the hearth, and he poured a cup for each of them before resuming his seat.

'Thank you for your hospitality, Lord De Lune,' Meryall said, taking a sip of her wine.

Lord De Lune looked at her with an air of confusion, frowning slightly. He shook his head almost imperceptibly and reached for his cup. Meryall knew that he would not remember her visit to him, but people sometimes retained some impression from their dream visitation, and she suspected that he was searching for a reason for some thought, feeling or glimpse of memory her presence summoned.

'You are quite welcome. I know that you have offered your services to the Allreds in their hour of need and thank you for your work in returning Aelcea Allred to health. I am of course eager to help in any way I can. However, I confess that I could not guess at the reason for your request to meet with me.'

Meryall bowed her head. 'You may not be aware, sir, that the body of a young man was found not far from our village some days ago – a young man by the name of Avery Greenhalgh.'

She watched his face – looking for his response. The lines of his face deepened into a frown, and he drew a deep sigh.

'I am sorry to hear it … I am acquainted with his sister, Eda. What happened to the young man?'

Meryall could not trace any signs of untruthfulness in his voice or manner, although she recollected that his experience in gambling and mercantile pursuits might mean that he was skilled in telling lies.

'He was stabbed several times – to the stomach and thigh, most likely with a thin-bladed dagger,' Madoc said, his deep voice steady and matter of fact.

Lord De Lune leaned back in his chair, his hands clasped before him.

'Does Eda know?' he asked.

'Yes,' Meryall said. 'We took word to her ourselves. We had hoped to assure ourselves of her safety, given the fate of her brother.'

'And did you find her well?' Lord De Lune said, his eyes fixed on Meryall's face.

'We found her safe. However, we also found that she had been the subject of a plot to do her harm – indeed we fear that the culprit intended to end her life.'

Lord De Lune leapt to his feet. 'Gods! Who? And for what purpose? Who made this attempt?' He paced the room, his fists clenched and face taut.

'We cannot establish why – but we have a fair indication that Richard Mangnall, the apothecary of this town, was the wrongdoer,' Meryall said.

She stood and poured fresh wine into his cup, placing it in his hands and gently signalling that he take his chair. He took the cup gratefully and threw himself into his chair, his efforts to regain his ironclad self-command clear in his heaving chest and shadowed brow. A long moment passed.

'And where is the apothecary now?' he said, his voice cold with anger.

'We are unsure. He was at the Sunn Inn when we arrived but appeared to take flight when he realised that we were there – knocking Avarall about the head in his bid to make good his escape. The sheriff of that place and his neighbours have sent out search parties. I doubt that he would come back here. He stated to Eda that he was passing through on his way to visit relatives in Ulnes Walton, but again, it seems likely that was not the truth.'

Meryall was careful to give a full account of what had been done. Lord De Lune was the sheriff of his township. They owed him as thorough a report as that they would provide to Wyot – now that they were as sure as it was possible to be that he had not been involved in the intrigues that they had uncovered. Lord De Lune sat drumming his fingers on the arm of his chair.

'I suppose that you suspected me of some villainy in Eda's case?'

Meryall assessed that he would respond better to a straightforward answer. 'I apologise, sir. The initial information we received from Avery was not promising – our subsequent conversation with Eda has made all clear – I can understand now that you were merely honouring Eda's wishes in refusing to tell Avery where she was.'

Lord De Lune met her eyes for a long moment. He smiled a little. 'And you must have made some remarkably discreet enquiries in order to trace Eda. I will not ask you who told you of her whereabouts, nor will I seek to chastise them. They did well by me, it seems, in helping to clear me of suspicion.'

'Indeed, it is a valuable servant who recognises where not following an order is necessary for the good of all,' Avarall said.

Meryall sipped at her wine, her thoughts occupied with the many twisting turns and loose ends in the case before her.

'What more can you tell us about Richard Mangnall and his family?' she asked, unsure of what value there was in asking, but unable to think of another path likely to yield useful information.

'His family were well known to mine. His mother, I believe, was widowed soon after she became pregnant with him. She remarried some time afterwards. The apothecary shop belonged to her, although after her death, it passed to Richard's stepfather, before coming into his hands on his stepfather's death. He has a sister – he told the truth when he mentioned relatives in Ulnes, for that is where she lives, but as you say, I find it difficult to believe that he has gone on to her house, given the nature of his mission. I cannot understand why he would wish to hurt Eda, it is incomprehensible – she is not linked to him in any way that I can see.'

His voice held a note of pain that Meryall was surprised to hear – she had not expected him to show much attachment to a woman he had bedded – he appeared to make such a regular habit of it that she had rather supposed that he cared not at all for any woman. Meryall judged that Eda had not made her pregnancy known to him and thought it best not to increase Lord De Lune's rage by making the extent of the apothecary's villainy clear to him – there was little benefit in sharing that knowledge now.

'What was your own knowledge and relationship with the apothecary?' she asked.

'We knew each other as boys. His mother and stepfather had served as apothecary to the castle, and I maintained this tradition, keeping Richard on as apothecary to my people when he took over the shop. I pass the time of day with him if I see him and share a cup of mead with him on the occasions when I am free when he visits to tend to someone or other within the walls. He has always been quiet, but genial and friendly in my dealings with him. I have not heard complaint of him from any of those in my household, either.'

Meryall placed her cup on the table before the fire and stood, the others following her lead. 'I am sorry to leave you with such ill news, sir. We plan to continue home and to confer with our sheriff, that we may formulate a plan for hunting him down. Men already search for him, but our experience of him thus far suggests that he is both resourceful and unpredictable.'

Lord De Lune acknowledged this with a short bow. 'I thank you all for your vigilance. I will be eager for word from any who have sight of that dog and will send out my own men in search of him also.'

The night air was cool on Meryall's cheeks, which were warmed by the wine and still more by the exertions of the conversation and disclosure to Lord De Lune, who had proven himself more passionate about the protection of his womenfolk than she had anticipated.

Chapter 15

Faron and Aelcea bid their guests farewell on a bright, crisp morning. The April sun was gaining in strength but was still hampered by the residue of a cold, damp night, the evidence of which showed itself in hanging mists, trapped in the closely leaved trees and bushes along their path. The lively, noisy river kept pace with them as they followed its curves away from the town and towards home. Their horses, who felt like familiar friends to Meryall after their long rides, were well-rested and well fed. Their contentment in the sunshine and their full bellies showed in the high steps of their hooves and the shakes they gave to their manes as they trod the well-worn road.

The horses would cover the distance – a little more than twenty miles of smooth road – without trouble and with luck they should arrive back in Thornton within an hour or so past noon, allowing for a rest for refreshments mid-morning.

The River Lune widened as they moved on, bringing the tang of the sea with its quick waters, a reminder that it broadened into an estuary as it met the north-easterly coast.

Their route lay inland, to meet the ford of the River Wyre at a narrow spot and Meryall found her heart lighter at the first glimpse of familiar land. The unresolved intrigues of the past few days lay heavily upon her, and she was looking forward to the welcome sight of her own garden and a night in her own bed. Meryall looked at the golden bursts of dandelions all along the verges. She must pick some when she got home – the dandelion was such a useful plant. The roots made a potent dream vision enhancing brew and the leaves a nutritious food, but the flowers produced a fine, rich golden wine, which carried the flavour of spring and helped to settle a quarrelsome stomach. But, before it was possible to focus on the comfortable concerns of home, there would need to be a good deal of discussion with the sheriff. Meryall smiled. Though weary and eager to be home, she would welcome the keenness of Wyot's mind and the warmth of his manner.

The village square was busy when they rode in. Meryall saw Katerin at their stand – she had left goods to be taken to market and was thankful that Katerin had spread them neatly alongside her own. She waved cheerily at her and made a note to herself that she would make Katerin a blackthorn threshold charm, by way of thanks for her kindness.

Everett was in the stable yard of the sheriff's compound when they arrived. He took their reins, promising to rub down the animals and feed them a handful of apples as payment for their labours. Meryall was hungry – it seemed a long time since they had stopped to eat a meagre share of oat bread, cheese and bacon mid-morning and she doubted not that her companions would also be ready for a meal. Wyot had not anticipated their arrival so soon, expecting them to dinner rather than to a late midday meal, but his kitchens were always well stocked, and the table soon groaned under an array of dishes. Avarall ate a hearty meal, which evidenced her full recovery, a fact that Madoc clearly did not miss and which added savour to both his and Meryall's own meals.

They sat so long in discussion that it was almost time for dinner when they had done with their talk. Meryall and Madoc declined to stay, but Wyot sent them away with a parcel from his kitchens, fearing that the cold hearth and store cupboards of a house empty since the last market day would provide little to cheer and fortify them. Meryall accepted with good grace, after unsuccessfully protesting that there was no need, as she had ample stocks of root vegetables and all manner of dried meats and preserves. Wyot escorted them to the outer hall door. 'What puzzles me most,' he said as they walked, 'is the difference in the manner of Avery's death and the apothecary's attempts on the lives of the two women. The apothecary seems the only feasible culprit in all of these cases and yet why kill Avery in such a brutal manner, which was guaranteed to attract attention?'

'Perhaps it was a matter of necessity,' Meryall replied. 'Without the time or opportunity for subtler measures, the apothecary may have been brought to rely on a faster and more brutal means of securing his ends. I, however, cannot fathom what his motivation was for wishing to harm these three people.'

Wyot sighed. 'Ah, it is a bad business. I thank you both for your exertions. It is unlikely we would know so much or be able to link these events without your endeavours.'

The company parted, Avarall having remained in the hall to eat her dinner with the sheriff and his deputies. Everett, Meryall noticed, had taken a seat at Avarall's elbow and was attending to her every word. Avarall did not appear to have noticed his earnest gaze.

The road from the village to Meryall's house was scarcely more than a mile and a half. Thornton Cleveleys was set back a little from the coast, and Meryall's way led further inland, through a stretch of marshy land which ended in a forested area. The path was growing dark but was so well known to them both that their feet carried them on with little need for light. The trees thinned as they approached Meryall's front gate and the sky opened out to a deep, dark blue scattered with stars.

The cave house sat in a sandstone cliff, and the chill of the stone hung about them as they entered. Madoc struck a match to the hearth, which lay ready for a fire, and the merry flames soon snatched at the cold fingers of the night. Meryall poured parsnip wine into a jug and placed cups on the little table by the hearth, pulling the two chairs closer together. It was most agreeable to be home.

They sat in companionable silence for a long time, the

wine working to still and relax their minds. Madoc was becoming sleepy when Meryall spoke.

'I think that as the day ways have not succeeded in locating the apothecary, I will dream walk tomorrow to search for him.'

Madoc rubbed Meryall's feet, as she rested them on his lap. 'I will come by after I close the shop and look in on you, then,' he replied. 'And I will bring dinner, for you will be tired and hungry after your journey.'

Meryall murmured agreement, weary and content.

Madoc had dressed, eaten and gone to his shop when Meryall awoke. She lay enjoying the feel of her own bed and listening to the birds in the woods around the cave house. Her garden would be in want of attention, but her priority today would be to journey in search of Richard Mangnall. She would welcome visitors for a few hours – it was likely that many people from the village would require her services after she had been absent for several days, but in the early afternoon, she would place a sign upon her door and make herself ready for her dream walk. She had plentiful supplies of the herbs she would need.

Of more immediate importance was a morning meal – she was ravenous. Meryall drew water from the wellspring which bubbled at the edge of her garden and set it to boil while she unpacked cheese and bread from Wyot's basket of provisions. The loaf had stiffened a little overnight, so Meryall set it to toast over the fire and spread it with butter and honey, adding a generous wedge of cheese to her plate.

Meryall provided services to many of her neighbours, who paid her in milk, butter, cheese, honey and many other foodstuffs.

Consequently, her larder was in general plentifully stocked. She was glad of the cheese from Wyot's basket, however. Wyot often hosted merchants from many countries, and she suspected that the soft, creamy cheese, encased in a white rind that she found in the basket, was the gift of a French merchant.

Meryall washed and dressed, pulling on a comfortable old gown of red cloth, kilting the skirts to her knees so that it would not drag in the mud of the garden.

Meryall admired Avarall's sleek silhouette in her fitted breeches but preferred the freedom of movement of a gown.

The air was fresh and stirred with a brisk breeze. Meryall stood at her gate and looked out into the forest around her. A crow landed on a tree nearby and gave a raucous caw, dipping his head and looking curiously at Meryall. She smiled.

The crow visited her often and was an esteemed magical ally in some of her more elaborate workings. She had not given him a name – he had one of his own, and it would have been disrespectful to provide him with another.

Meryall had brought the crusts of her bread from her breakfast with her and unlatching the gate to pass into the lane, she placed them on a log, sitting at the other end to watch as the crow ate his breakfast.

She explained to him her plan for the day – that she

would be dream walking and why. The crow continued his meal but kept one sparkling black eye turned towards her as he ate.

He called a rough cry of acknowledgement for the food and the message, then hopped and stretched his wings to fly back to his post in an oak tree.

Meryall's days away from home had put her behind in her work. She had charms to make – including her promised threshold charm for Katerin.

Meryall took a red thread beaded with rowan berries (threaded fresh and now dry) and measured it out against her hand.

When she had a sufficient length, she carefully used another length of red thread to secure it to a circle of hawthorn twigs, whispering words to set the intention of the amulet.

She then took long, sharp blackthorns and tied them at intervals to two lengths of thread, fixing these in a cross shape across the centre of the rowan and hawthorn circlet, so that the thorns formed a barbed barrier across the aperture, whispering her verse once more as her fingers worked nimbly at the strings.

Meryall held up the finished piece and for a third time told the charm of its purpose.

She wrapped it in a scrap of brown paper, writing Katerin's name upon it and set it aside – it was likely that Katerin would drop in with her unsold stock and takings from the market in the course of the morning.

Meryall heard her gate open and close and looked up to

see a young woman from the village. She had been to visit previously in want of divination, hoping to be told that she would find a good man to settle with and have children. Meryall considered that people had little need of prophecy in cases such as this.

The people we are meant to find on our path find us without the need for guidance, but she knew that her words acted as reassurance and would help the young woman to feel content in the knowledge that all would be as it was meant to be.

Meryall's role as the cunning woman for the village was often as much about offering a listening ear and a reassuring word as about the more arcane practices of divination, charm making and hex breaking.

Meryall welcomed the young woman and placed the kettle upon the hearth and herbs in the pot. She cast a handful of dragon's claw leaves on the fire and breathed in the smoke.

In cases such as this, she would ask that she be given the guidance that was needed, rather than an answer to the question asked. People were seldom wise enough to ask the right questions.

Meryall saw a road rise up in her vision and the crow soaring off into the distance. She walked ahead and felt a tug of tension. She looked down – a red thread had been stretched across the path and had snapped when she walked into it.

Meryall frowned. This message was not intended for her guest, this was a warning from the gods. Meryall halted on the track and looked ahead. The skies in the distance were stormy, and the crow had vanished from sight. The vision world shifted away. She was confused and disorientated. Meryall refocused her eyes on the flames, trying to find a way back in, but the flames refused to open to her.

Her guest looked at her expectantly. Meryall took a deep breath and forced herself to smile, taking a sip of her tisane to steady herself, inventing a message of reassurance for the young woman.

The young woman left content, happy to consider that her love would come and that it was only a matter of time.

Meryall did not hear Katerin's rap at the door and started with surprise when she opened the door, calling a greeting.

She could not tell how long she had been sitting, although the pot at her side had grown cold.

'Does something ail you?' Katerin asked, her hand on Meryall's shoulder.

'No, I simply allowed my thoughts to carry me away,' Meryall replied. 'I have been looking forward to seeing you!' Her tone was bright to throw off the gloom of her thoughts. 'I made you a gift by way of thanks for your services in taking my goods to market.'

'I need no thanks, Meryall!' Katerin chided her. 'There have been many times when you have done likewise for me.'

Meryall smiled. 'My pot has grown cold – can I offer you wine?'

Katerin accepted the offer and seated herself at the table, pulling the unsold stock and a little bag of coins from a bag and placing them on the dresser. 'You made a good profit and sold out of protection charms.'

'They always sell well. I will make some more for next time.'

She took an earthenware bottle from her cupboard – the cork was held in place with a string, deftly bound about the neck. Meryall cut the string with her pocket knife and removed the cork, which emerged with a mild pop, followed by the scent of rich, dark elderberries.

Katerin sniffed. 'Ah! My favourite. You are too kind.'

'I feel in need of a restorative. It will do both of us good,' Meryall said.

The two women sat in comfortable silence, the warmth of the wine spreading through their throats and chests.

'What put you into such deep thought?' Katerin asked eventually.

Meryall sighed. 'I have a dream walk to take, in search of someone who has done considerable harm ... the vision I was given by the gods, unsought, seemed to warn me not to journey along that path. Yet I know not what else is to be done.'

'What will you do?' Katerin asked.

'I will go – but I will take heed of the warning and ask for protection on my way.'

'Then I will stay here until you return,' Katerin said.

Meryall smiled. 'No need, Madoc will come after his shop closes.'

'That is a long while yet. I will stay, tend the fire and make a good dinner for you both for your return.'

Meryall hugged her fondly. 'Thank you, that is most

kind. I will be gone some time, do not fret about me.'

Gathering her supplies and leaving Katerin in the kitchen, Meryall stepped through to the bedroom. She opened the window and gave a shrill whistle.

She heard an answering caw in the trees and knew that the crow had heard and understood. She prepared herself to dream walk, drinking her tisane, casting a circle, arranging the herb garland and tying her red thread to the bedpost and her wrist.

Meryall lay down and looked up at the whitewashed stone ceiling of the cave house, which rose in a smooth curve above her.

She had grown up in Horn Cottage and had always loved the comforting solidity of the stone around her, with its traces of the hands of her ancestors upon every surface.

The herbs began to lift her, and she closed her eyes and found herself once again in her spirit place – her other cave, this one raw and pulsing with power. Meryall focused on Richard Mangnall, calling him to mind as she had seen him in his apothecary shop, recalling the feeling of his presence.

She drew an outline of a man on the mud with the point of a stick and as she had done many times, spat in the earth and dabbed her forehead with the claylike mixture.

Meryall stood and stepped outside the cave, looking into the shadowy woods. She whistled to the crow and heard his hoarse reply close at hand. He landed in a swirl of glossy black wings to perch on a stump nearby. Meryall smiled in relief, thanking the crow for his presence on her journey.

'This may be a difficult journey, crow,' she said.

The crow hopped and tilted his head in reply.

She bowed to him. 'When you are ready, so am I.'

The crow stretched his wings and swooped up to a tree in a path to the right. Meryall followed.

The crow flew on, stopping to perch on tree trunks and low branches within Meryall's sight, looking back to check that she continued to follow.

Though it had been daytime when she set out in the waking world, it was night-time in this place, and a mist hung in the trees. Meryall pulled her gown close.

She had left her fox-hooded cloak in the sacred cave and felt a biting cold that she had rarely been conscious of when walking in these woods. There was a whoosh of pressure in the air around Meryall.

The crow gave a loud rattling caw of alarm and the mist closed in on her, pushing the breath from her chest and making her feel faint. The thick fog tasted of mould and dark, damp places as it filled her mouth and nose.

Meryall could not tell whether the increasing darkness around her was born of the mist, or whether it was faintness stealing upon her, but she could neither move nor cry out. She fell to her knees, the forest floor soft beneath her, and felt a faint snap, as the red thread at her wrist broke away.

Meryall opened her eyes. A tawny twilight fog surrounded her, but the floor beneath her was no longer the soft, fragrant forest floor, but bare earth, barren and featureless.

Meryall opened her mouth and shouted to the crow. Her voice seemed to come from a great distance, and it cost her much effort to call out. Meryall heard the crow caw in reply, but his call came from so far away that she could not tell in which direction to turn.

Meryall rose to her feet, looking around her. She could see nothing around her: no paths, features or objects to help her make sense of her surroundings.

Meryall shivered. It was cold in this place beyond places. She had misjudged Richard Mangnall and dangerously underestimated him. He was powerful and knowledgeable in the art of travelling beyond the body.

She had heard from her mother, who had been a renowned cunning woman, that some people were able to protect themselves from unwanted visits from dream walkers, casting a glamour on the walker, turning them from their path. She tried to remember if her mother had told her of a way for a lost walker to return but found that the cold slowed her mind. She fought the rising terror – she must keep moving and stay awake, or else she would sleep forever…

Chapter 16

Katerin was uneasy. She had busied herself in preparing a stew, which simmered gently over the fire. Two hours had passed since Meryall had gone. She opened the door cautiously and walked over to the bed once again. Meryall lay still, her chest moving so little that for a moment Katerin thought that she was no longer breathing. Katerin took Meryall's hand. It was cold and lay limp against her warm palm.

Katerin pulled a warm woollen blanket over Meryall, careful not to displace the garland of herbs around her and went to feed the fire. She could think of little to do but watch over her friend and keep her warm until Madoc arrived – she did not wish to leave Meryall alone.

It seemed a long time until she heard the front door latch, although it could scarcely have been an hour. She stepped through to meet Madoc, relieved that her lone vigil had ended, but unhappy to be the bearer of such troubling news.

Madoc listened quietly to Katerin's account of the length of time Meryall had wandered and what Katerin had done to keep her warm and comfortable. When she had finished, he rose to his feet, pulling his cloak back on.

'Trickle a little mead from a sponge into her mouth every so often and ensure the fire does not go out. I must ride to Poltun to find Master Arledge.'

Katerin nodded. 'Farewell, Madoc, may the gods speed your journey.'

Katerin knew that Poltun was no more than three miles away. Madoc would need to borrow a horse for the journey, having none of his own. She calculated that even if he found a horse quickly and had no difficulty in locating and bringing Master Arledge back with him, it would be above an hour and a half before he returned. It felt like a long time to continue alone, unsure of where Meryall wandered and what perils she might be facing. She wished she had thought to ask Madoc to send word to her husband on the way through the village.

She had met Master Arledge only once when she was a girl and visiting a family member who was unwell in Poltun. He had seemed old to her then, so she imagined that he must be ancient now. Katerin realised that Meryall had no clock in the house and that it was too far from the village to hear the ring of the town hall clock tower.

She took a bowl from the sideboard and found a sponge on the shelf amongst the jars of herbs, potions and charms. She opened the deep cupboard carved into the stone that served as a larder and storeroom.

Meryall had many bottles of her homemade wines, in addition to those gifted to her by friends and neighbours.

They were neatly labelled and arranged, and Katerin quickly found a bottle of mead.

She poured a small amount of the golden liquid into the bowl and another measure into a cup for herself, to help warm her heart and keep her calm during her vigil.

Katerin was just trickling the first dose of mead into Meryall's mouth, careful not to get the sticky liquid onto her chin, when she heard a tap at the door, followed by the creak of its opening. She stiffened. It was too soon for Madoc to have returned.

'Katerin?' It was the sheriff's voice.

She sagged with relief. 'In here,' she called in reply.

Wyot came through to the bedroom, his kind eyes filled with concern. He greeted Katerin, clapping a hand on her shoulder and squeezing it. 'I am come to keep you company on your watch. I have sent a man with Madoc along with an extra horse for Master Arledge. They will be here as swiftly as they are able. In the meantime, I had Avarall drop into your house to acquaint Randall with the situation.'

'Thank you. I neglected to ask Madoc to speak to him.'

Katerin was cheered by the sheriff's presence and the briskness in his tone.

'I daresay Madoc was too full of worry when he left here to recollect, but by the time he had walked into the village to find me, his plan was fully formed and detailed. He had not forgotten you. How is she?' Wyot stepped to Meryall's side.

Katerin shrugged. 'There has been no change. She breathes, but shallowly and she is so cold! There seems to be nothing I can do to warm her. I am warming stones in the fire at present to wrap in cloth and place about her.'

'Did she leave any instruction for what you were to do in these circumstances?'

Katerin sighed. 'No, although she acknowledged that she was worried about this walk. She had talked with the crow who lives near Horn Cottage, to ask that he guide her.'

Wyot went to the window, opening the shutter to the light and air of the late afternoon. A crow sat in the tree near to the garden fence.

'Can you take the crow something to eat, Katerin?'

Katerin found a piece of bread and spread it with lard. She took the bread outside and placed it on the gatepost. The crow swept down and landed on the post, taking up the bread in his talons and pecking at it. Katerin stood watching him eat. The crow paid her little attention.

She had seldom seen a crow at such close quarters and admired the blue sheen of his feathers in the golden afternoon light. His beak and talons were dark as jet and of fearsome sharpness, yet he picked at the morsel of bread with delicacy and precision.

'She needs you; she's lost, I think,' Katerin whispered to the crow.

He lifted his head for a moment and regarded her steadily, before continuing with his meal. Katerin sighed, wiped her hands on her apron and turned towards the house.

Wyot and Katerin sat at the scarred-oak kitchen table, the bedroom door propped open so that they could watch over Meryall, as they ate the stew Katerin had prepared for

Meryall and Madoc to eat when she returned from her journey and he returned from his shop. Their mood sombre, and although it was savoury and well-flavoured, neither of them could do justice to the food before them. Katerin paused with her spoon raised.

'Have you met Master Arledge?' she asked, keen to break the long, anxious silence.

'Yes, on many occasions. He was a close friend of Meryall's mother and father.'

'I never knew her father,' Katerin said. 'She seldom mentions him, either.'

'He was a good man but died at sea when Meryall was but a small child. It was a great affliction to both Meryall and her mother – it is small wonder that she does not speak of him.'

'Master Arledge is a highly respected cunning man, I believe,' Katerin said, remembering her mother speaking of him.

'Yes, he is renowned for his skills and is believed to be uncommonly powerful. I am confident that he will be able to help Meryall,' Wyot replied.

They sat at the table for a long time, their wait punctuated only by Katerin's frequent checks on Meryall.

Wyot did not voice his conviction that if Arledge could not help Meryall, she was beyond help, for fear of distressing Katerin, yet this thought came back to his mind repeatedly as the long minutes went by.

Katerin stood up suddenly – hand outstretched for silence and eyes fixed on the door. Wyot's ears could trace no sound from the forest, but seeing Katerin listening intently, he rose and went to the front gate. He stood looking into the distance for some time before he was able to hear and begin to see the outlines of mounted men amongst the trees. The dusk was drawing in, and he could not make out their faces until they were close to the cottage.

He smiled and called a loud halloo. He heard Madoc's rich, deep voice in an echoing shout. Impatient, Wyot walked down the path to meet the party.

Madoc, mounted on one of Wyot's ponies, was flushed from the crisp forest air and his haste. Avarall rode behind him and to his right rode a spare figure wrapped in a dark cloak. Wyot shook Madoc by the hand and threw his arm around his shoulders in greeting.

When the cloaked man had dismounted, he turned and made a short bow.

'Master Arledge,' he said. The man drew back his hood. His white hair hung in a long plait over his shoulder. He wore a dense snowy beard, but despite his age, his eyes were a burning, intense blue and his expression was intelligent and kind. He smiled at Wyot and moved forward to embrace him.

'Ah, Wyot! You have grown into an impressive man. You were a skinny boy when I saw you last.'

Wyot laughed. 'If by impressive you mean well fed, then you are quite right.'

Arledge chuckled. 'Enjoy it while it lasts. Age can gnaw the flesh from your bones, believe me.'

Wyot greeted Avarall, giving her a quick hug of gratitude. 'We must go within,' he said gravely. 'There has been no change since Madoc left.'

Arledge grimaced, gesturing for Wyot to lead the way.

Katerin lit a rushlight and placed it on the table in the bedroom. Arledge seated himself on the edge of the bed. He put his hand on Meryall's forehead and closed his eyes. After a few moments, he withdrew his hand and opened his eyes. Madoc looked at him questioningly.

'I would be grateful if someone would boil the kettle for a brew of linden flowers. Meryall – and all of us – will benefit from a cup when she returns.'

Madoc went into the kitchen, seeming happier to be busy with something. The thought of Meryall wandering alone in a place beyond this world, perhaps unable to return, had run through all of them like ice. Master Arledge's calm and activity filled the group with a sense of hope.

In the bedroom beyond, Arledge took a lump of wax from his bag, warming it in front of the fire for a few moments. When it was malleable, he shaped it into a little figure. Arledge took out scissors and snipped a tiny piece of fabric from the inner hem of Meryall's red gown.

He wrapped the scrap around the poppet, binding it with a hair plucked from her head.

He called Katerin to him. 'You mentioned that there is a crow that Meryall called upon for help?'

'Yes, we gave him food a little while ago.'

Arledge patted her arm. 'That was well done, for we must ask something of him now.'

Arledge walked to the front gate. He gave a long whistling call and heard the crow's rattling tone answering him. The crow flew to a tree near the gate. Arledge bowed solemnly to him.

'Master Crow. I have need of a token from you to help return Meryall from her wandering.'

The crow gave a caw of acknowledgement and took flight.

Katerin watched, puzzled. 'Will he not help, then?' she said.

Arledge patted her arm. 'Patience, he will return.'

They stood waiting for some moments. Katerin gave a start – the crow was returning, with something dark in his beak.

He flew over them and dropped the object – it fluttered in a spiralling arc to the ground at their feet. Arledge called his thanks to the sky – the crow was nowhere to be seen – and picked up the long black feather from the ground.

On Meryall's long, well-used table, Arledge lay the little wax figure down. He took a length of red thread and bound the figure to the feather, whispering words beyond Katerin's hearing as he worked.

He took up the figure and placed it in Meryall's left hand, folding it under her right hand upon her breast. There was a long expectant silence.

At a gesture from Arledge, they retired to the kitchen table. Madoc took cups from the sideboard and a pot of honey from the store cupboard and poured the sweet, fragrant tisane.

'Now,' said Arledge, raising his hands in a gesture of supplication to the gods, 'we can only wait.'

Chapter 17

Meryall could not tell how long she had walked through the barren, befogged land of the place beyond places. She fought hard to stay focused.

The mist seeped into her mind, making her brain feel slow and her body heavy and cumbersome. Meryall dropped to her knees for what appeared to be the hundredth time.

The ground felt so welcoming, she wanted to press her face into it and remain there, sleeping. She pushed herself to her feet. She could not go to sleep here. She needed to go home. Back to Horn Cottage. The atmosphere around her cleared abruptly.

Meryall took a deep, shuddering breath. Clarity returned to her with the freshness of the air. She could smell the forest. Meryall heard the call of the crow. She concentrated on the sound – it came from her left, and she walked towards it, the path clearing as she moved toward the crow's calls. Her eyes filled with tears of relief and she whispered thanks to the crow.

Beneath her feet, Meryall felt the ground grow soft.

Looking down, she saw old leaves and pine needles. She could make out the outline of trees ahead of her.

Meryall followed the crow into the woods, winding her way through their welcome shelter until she found her sacred cave space. She stepped inside, tired beyond anything she had ever experienced. She seated herself by the fire and closed her eyes. She felt the familiar sensation of growing huge, expanding beyond her body. There was an odd pull at her consciousness, and she caught a brief glimpse of Richard Mangnall. He sat, eyes closed and mouth shaping a soundless incantation. His face was drawn into a taut, snarling mask. Above his bowed head, Meryall could see the arched, buff-toned rock of a limestone cave. With a jolt, Meryall realised that she knew where he was.

She gave a laugh of triumph, then woke abruptly, confused by the sensation of the sound in her throat as she returned to her body. Meryall lay for a moment, feeling her strength and essence returning to her body. Her head ached, and she felt chilled to her soul, but she was home.

Many miles away, Richard Mangnall sat before a low, dying fire. Its light barely reached the stone sides and ceiling of the cave, but the warmth of the flames still gave some comfort. He looked pale and thin in the fading light, his eyes shadowed and his lips dry. He had not slept for more than an hour or two for some days and had eaten only sparingly. The lack of sleep made his eyes feel gritty. He rubbed them with the heels of his palms, pulling his hands away abruptly and jumping at the sudden crackle of sap in the firewood. He could not recall feeling at once so tired and so on edge. It was an unpleasant state to be in. His thoughts raced, his heart thumped too quickly and too hard in his ribcage, and his stomach felt like a tight, sour knot.

It was hard to comprehend how things had gone so badly wrong and yet Richard was not surprised – there was an inevitability to it all.

It was his lot to suffer and to be denied his due. He grasped his hands together in front of him, pressing his fingers against one another until his knuckles whitened, as if in frantic, fervent prayer. He had taken action to ensure that Meryall could not find him, and yet…

He knew they were coming. He had always known that they would. Anger flooded through him – he had planned so carefully, and all had been going well until they came to Lune. They had interfered in his plans – had brought with them doubts and scrutiny and their intrusive interest in matters that did not concern them, and they had ruined him. His rage subsided quickly and left only sadness and crushing fatigue.

He took a thick book from the leather pack at his side. The spine of the book was worn and the pages were thin with age and use. The book crawled with a cramped, spiky hand which rushed over the pages between splotches of ink and blots. His mother's handwriting. This had been her journal and contained much of her knowledge.

Richard felt the complex mix of emotions that his mother always evoked in him as he ran his hand over the carved leather cover, tracing the well-known motif of ivy leaves. He turned to a random passage and began to read.

'—though he has talent, he is weak and unable to forge it into the power that should be his birthright. It is well that he is not heir to his true father's estate, for he is not worthy of it.'

Richard gave a bitter laugh and searched through the pages until he found a section entitled 'the hawthorn path'.

He took a stick and stirred up the fire to give more light and settled himself more comfortably on the hard stone floor to read.

Everyone had rushed into her bedroom, crowding around her bed, until Arledge had stilled them with a benign wave of his hand, while he examined her.

Declaring her well enough to rise, he had allowed Meryall to take a seat at the kitchen table. Arledge, Madoc, Wyot and Avarall were seated around her, relief plain on their faces. Katerin had hugged her before she returned home, grateful that Meryall had made it back safely, but fatigued and eager to be in her husband's arms.

'This apothecary is a powerful man,' Arledge said, his face thoughtful. 'Great care must be taken in how you approach your next steps.'

'I underestimated him once, that is enough. He is not aware that I saw him as I was pulled back to my body. The place I saw was the Fairy Holes Cavern. It is an ancient, sacred place, but also on high ground and readily defensible.'

Wyot sighed. 'It is outside of my jurisdiction and moreover a long ride, taking us through the Forest of Bowland. I am friendly with the sheriff of Whitewell Manor, the nearest place to the cavern, but I fear that by the time we reach it, this Richard Mangnall may have moved on.'

Arledge frowned. 'Mangnall? That is his name?'

Wyot nodded, puzzled.

Arledge looked keenly at Meryall. 'Do you know his mother's name?'

Meryall shook her head. 'No. I only know that his mother took over the running of the apothecary shop and ran it until she died when it passed to Richard's stepfather. The name above the door is S. Helm. I believe that may have been his father's name.'

Arledge shook his head. 'That was her father's name. Sitha Mangnall was a cunning woman of great repute. I remember her well. She was powerful, one of the few people left who held knowledge that has almost died out now.'

'It appears that she taught Richard many of her skills and yet we were told that the village of Lune has been without cunning folk for some years,' Meryall said.

'Why would Richard have chosen to practise as an apothecary rather than as a cunning man?' Madoc asked.

Arledge shrugged. 'His mother was a formidable woman. I cannot imagine that she was a patient teacher. Perhaps he rejected her teaching in rebellion.'

'Did not Lord De Lune tell us that Richard's mother and then his stepfather had served as apothecary to the town of Lune?' Avarall queried.

'Indeed, we were informed that it was the family business in the town,' Meryall agreed.

'Sitha was not originally from Lune,' Arledge said. 'She came from the town of Ulnes.'

Wyot caught at the name. 'Ulnes? Did the apothecary not mention to Eda that he had relatives there?'

'Yes – Lord De Lune confirmed that he has a sister living there,' Meryall said. 'But this brings us no closer to understanding why Lune has been without cunning folk for so long, despite a skilled cunning man living within the town.'

Wyot rose from the table. 'That may need to be a question for another day. I propose we ride for Whitewell at first light to see if we can trace him there. I will send word to Lord De Lune of our plans.'

All were in agreement and parted for the night, with Arledge returning to the town at Wyot's invitation. Meryall knew he would be handsomely accommodated there and did not object, although she longed to talk more with him.

Their guests departed, Madoc and Meryall sat in the sudden quietness of the cottage. Madoc pulled Meryall into a tight embrace, his face pressed against her hair. She leaned into his warmth and the familiarity of his broad shoulders, chest and arms, profoundly weary and filled with an odd sensation of greyness, as if the fog of the place beyond places still hung about her. She gave Madoc a gentle squeeze, and he let her go, understanding that she needed to move away.

Meryall pulled her cloak about her and took a jug and a few small items from the dresser. 'I am going to get water; I will be back shortly.'

Madoc gave a parting wave of his hand and sat down beside the fire, his face tired and drawn.

The forest was quiet in the crisp early evening air, a gentle breeze setting the leaves on the trees whispering. Meryall walked out of the cottage gate and cut through the trees half a mile back towards the village, into the darkness cast by the densely packed trunks. As she walked on, little patches of colour showed up against the dark trees. Rags fluttered from branches, little flags made up of old shirts, gowns or cloaks.

At the centre of the ring of bedecked trees, the ground dropped away into a small rock face on one side, in the middle of which was a sparkling pool. Water trickled down the rocks, making many tiny needle-like waterfalls, pouring down onto a ledge of rock cushioned by a soft, velvet green moss, shining with glimmers of phosphorescence, before the water trailed into the pool. Meryall knelt on a flat rock at the edge of the water. The quiet trickle of the rivulets falling onto the stone was a peaceful sound, and she closed her eyes, listening to the water and feeling the ancient energy of the place.

Opening her eyes, Meryall drank a little of the water from the cup of her hands, savouring the sweetness and purity, then splashed her face three times. She took a strip of material from her belt pouch; it was a rag she had cut from an old cloak of hers to use to clean with, but it would suffice for a healing charm, as it belonged to her. She dipped the cloth into the water. Raising it up, she passed the damp scrap over her face, touching it to her forehead, the crown of her head and her heart. Rising from her knees, she walked to the nearest tree – an oak with a vast, spreading canopy.

Meryall reached into the lower branches and tied the strip (loosely, so as not to harm the tree) to a slender sprig. As the cloth dried, the power of the well would heal the owner. Meryall hoped that the after-effects from her dream walk would fade as the fabric dried – she had never returned from a dream walk so jaded. Already, the purity of the place and the deep peace that resided there had eased the feelings of tiredness and heaviness that encompassed her.

Meryall sat wrapped in the stillness of the clearing for a long time. Rubbing her legs, stiff from her cold, hard seat on the stone, she was conscious of an abrupt prickling static in the air. Looking up, she saw a cloaked figure before her. She smiled in relief.

'I see that you have not lost the trick of moving quietly, Arledge,' she said.

Arledge pushed back his hood and stepped forward, grinning boyishly. 'I just wanted to remind you of some of the skills you have yet to learn.'

Meryall rolled her eyes good-naturedly. 'Of course, I am but a novice in the cunning arts.'

Arledge looked back at her, serious now. 'You have much natural skill, Meryall, you know that. Your divination is peerless … but I fear that you lack the skills that keep the cunning folk safe. The day-to-day business of serving your village is not the boundary of the cunning ways.'

Meryall looked into Arledge's face. She had known him when she was a child, and in her eyes, he had changed little. Even then, he had been white-haired and lined, but now, as then, he was strong and upright. And yet, he must be old.

'I have been talking with Madoc,' she said softly. 'He tells me that young Turi is growing in skill and may be happy for an opportunity to look after Thornton Cleveleys.'

Arledge inclined his head. 'I am sure if you wished to come and learn with me for a season, Turi could manage very well – and may appreciate being free of an exacting old man for a while!'

Meryall smiled. It might be pleasant to give time to learning again. She held a hope in her heart that there may also be the opportunity to travel with Madoc for a while if Turi was willing to look after the village for her. Meryall turned her thoughts to Richard Mangnall and his unhappy apprenticeship to his own mother.

'Do you know who Richard's father was?' she asked Arledge, frowning as she tried to remember if this had been mentioned by anyone she had spoken to.

Arledge shrugged. 'Sitha was her own woman. I cannot recall that there was talk of her settling with anyone before she met Richard's stepfather. She was a handsome woman, regal and haughty.'

Meryall was thoughtful. 'Do you think there is a chance that the late Lord De Lune may be Richard's father?'

Arledge tilted his head in thought. 'I never heard of it, but it would be very like Sitha to have set her sights on the lord of the castle.'

Meryall steepled her fingers before her, looking down at her nails. She began to suspect that the present Lord De Lune may be more intimately connected to Richard

Mangnall than he was aware. 'It is cold out here, Arledge. We should head home, though it has been pleasant to talk with you.'

Arledge laughed heartily. 'You head home, Meryall, I will see you tomorrow.' His eyes twinkled as he faded from the clearing.

Meryall blinked. I must be tired, she thought. I should have noticed that Arledge's physical form was not here at all. She shook her head, laughing. Another way for the old man to remind her of the skills she had yet to learn.

Meryall knelt to fill her jug at the pool and walked slowly back to the house. The dark woods smelled of the freshness of spring, and there was a hint of fox in the air. Meryall stopped and looked up at the moon. It was a fat crescent – almost a half-moon, vivid against the clear night sky. She gave a prayer of thanks for her return as she gazed up. I must make an offering to the crow, she reminded herself, although he had been mightily well fed that day!

Meryall unlatched the door and stepped into the warmth of the cottage. The stone walls radiated the heat of the fire and Meryall felt wrapped in the deep sense of home that the cave house held for her. Madoc's boots were placed neatly in front of the fire, and she could hear his soft, even breathing. She pulled off her own boots, hung up her cloak and undressed, folding her clothes neatly on the chest at the foot of the bed. She slid under the blankets and sank into the sweet-scented softness of sleep.

Chapter 18

Dawn found the party assembled at the sheriff's stables. Wyot had sent a boy on ahead to his counterpart at Whitewell as a courtesy and to ensure that additional support would be available if needed.

Arledge hugged Meryall, smiling as he looked at her face. 'You look well-rested. Do you feel better?'

She nodded and returned his smile.

Arledge looked at the handsome woman in front of him. He remembered Meryall visiting his house as a small child, running around his stone cottage with its shaggy, spidery thatch while he shared charms and recipes with her mother. She had loved exploring the trinkets and curios that Arledge had amassed and asked him endless questions about the many places he had visited as a young man. If he could persuade her to come and stay with him this winter, he knew that she would enjoy the books and artefacts he had collected from the wise folk and sacred places he had been.

Arledge put his hand in his pocket and pulled out a small leather pouch.

'I have something for you … an amulet to help keep you safe, given that you seem to be prone to getting into scrapes at present,' he said, putting the pouch into her hands.

Meryall smiled and kissed the old man on the cheek. She opened the pouch and found a scrap of dark green silk cushioning a small golden pendant. She lifted it up and looked closely at it. The pendant had the look of an old coin – it was embossed with a crescent moon with a star within and looked ancient.

'It's beautiful! Where did you get it?' she asked as she opened the clasp of the chain and put the necklace around her neck.

'I bartered for it with a privateer when I was travelling in the West Indian Ocean. I believe that he found it in a chest of treasures in a cave somewhere thereabouts, so there is no telling from whence it came originally … but I felt that it held the protective power of the moon, and it is a pretty trinket.'

Meryall lifted the pendant from her neck to admire it again. 'How many seas has it crossed to reach me?' she said, a look of longing on her face.

'Many, my dear, many,' Arledge replied with a chuckle.

'Thank you, I shall treasure it,' Meryall said.

She kissed the old man's cheek and moved to the pony Wyot had assigned her to check the length of the stirrups.

Arledge watched her for a moment, looking beyond her physical self to assess whether she carried any damage from her misadventure. She was perhaps not as robust as usual, but well and free from the remnants of the hooks that the apothecary had cast to ensnare her and prevent her spirit from returning to her body. The wounds that these hooks could leave on the soul, he knew from experience, could be long-lasting and could fester, imparting a cold, muted quality to the bearer of the injured soul.

Arledge tried to recall how many years it had been since Meryall's mother had passed. Perhaps ten. Or even twelve? Her mother's passing had interrupted her training.

Although Meryall was skilled in divination, charms and dream walking, ancient and little-known knowledge had died with her mother and Arledge grieved the fact that he had not been able to take the place of her mother, in ensuring that this old knowing lived on in Meryall. However, he was unable to leave his village and home to support Meryall often.

In many ways, Arledge thought, Meryall and Richard Mangnall were similarly situated. The apothecary's mother had also been a formidable cunning woman – she had held knowledge that even the older cunning folk shied away from – the shadow side of their work.

However, it was better that learning lived on – if only to inform future generations of practices which may be unsafe or unethical that they may otherwise stumble across accidentally, in the inevitable adventuring of young cunning folk.

Wyot laid a respectful hand on Arledge's elbow, interrupting his train of thought.

'May Avarall help you mount, sir?' he said quietly.

Arledge shook his head, throwing a puckish smile at

Avarall, who waited for his instruction. 'I am not so old just yet, Wyot,' he said, mildly.

Mounted and briefed on their route and plan, they set off. Avarall rode ahead, followed by Wyot and Arledge, Meryall and Madoc behind them and Everett riding at their heels. It was a defensive grouping that allowed a view of the road ahead and a sharp eye and a strong hand to the rear.

Their way would initially follow the curves of the River Wyre, from its broad sweep around Skippool to a thin trickle near Great Eccleston, where a web of little streams spread out. The road would enter the Forest of Bowland, a wild place which was home to boar and other such creatures, amongst thick ancient trees.

Avarall and Everett were uneasy about this section of their route – at the riverside, the land was open, and by keeping the water to one side, they had a natural defence, however, in the forest, the dense cover made the party vulnerable.

Meryall looked half amused by the warriors' caution around encountering a single man and ventured to mention that as far as they knew, Richard Mangnall had acted alone. Avarall had frowned at this and replied that even a single man might cause much damage from thick cover with projectile weapons, without having to venture close to them. They planned to join the River Hodder for part of the forest journey, which made their route longer but took them through open land.

They maintained a brisk pace, their sturdy ponies able to keep a good speed over the even paths along the river; their riders had little baggage to ensure that their load was as light as possible. The miles wore away well, and they had gone almost sixteen miles when they reached the village of Inglewhite mid-morning. It was a pleasant village, with a pretty pool on the green.

Wyot, who appeared to know at least one person in every location for some miles around, secured them a meal of fresh bread, chunks of roasted meat and apples, with long draughts of crisp spring water, from the kitchens of the inn.

Their horses grazed the sweet grass around the pool and drank their fill, watched by a flotilla of curious ducks. It was soon time to go on.

The innkeeper put chunks of rich, oaty tharf cake, wrapped in a piece of cloth, into their hands for the journey.

Meryall glanced at Madoc. They had done a good deal of riding lately, which they were not accustomed to. She hoped that he had brought a muscle salve with him, as her thighs and back were beginning to ache fiercely and they had many more miles to travel. Madoc caught her glance and reached out to squeeze her hand, touching it to his lips in a hasty kiss before they remounted.

The road remained open for some miles more before they entered the straggling hem of the forest. Avarall and Everett were immediately alert and watchful. The trees grew closer and closer together as they pressed on, the light of the fresh day dimmed by the rich canopy of leaves above and around them. Oak, holly, ash and beech trees soared high above them, wreathed in ivy. Old, twisted yew trees sent out branches like crooked fingers from trunks gnarled with age and filled with eye-shaped knots.

The river flowed at their side for some miles, but their path turned inwards for a while at this point of the track, taking them deeper into the forest.

The forest path came to a crossroads. Arledge raised his hand and called to Avarall to halt. The rest of the party came to a stop – watchful but puzzled by the old man's command. He dismounted and motioned Meryall to join him. The centre of the crossed paths was under an arc of greenery. Arledge pointed to the ground at the intersecting point of the track. Little round seeds studded the ground.

'What is it?' Meryall asked.

Arledge pointed up to the tree. 'This hawthorn has spilt its berries onto the crossroads for many years. The berries have been walked into the path by generations of feet passing this way. I have seen this happen once before – we must find a way around.'

Wyot and Madoc had dismounted and joined them.

'Why?' Wyot said, frowning at the path.

'The hawthorn helps us connect to other realms,' Arledge replied. 'Here, that power has been combined with the energy of the crossroads – where worlds meet. It is a powerful place. Under normal circumstances, I would suggest crossing with respect and acknowledging the worlds we pass between in this place, as the hawthorn is a powerful protector to those who seek its patronage … however, given our experience with the apothecary, I would suggest we take another path, for, with the manipulation of his magic, these crossroads could become a place of danger for us.'

Avarall too dismounted, curious, to look at the path with its surface, the berry stones of many years pressed into the earth like tiny cobblestones. Everett remained on his horse, keeping watch.

A loud cracking sound like that of a whip shook the air, followed by a flash of lightning. Birds rose up in the air all around them, filling the sky with the sound of their whirring wings and their agitated alarm calls. Everett's horse started forward in fright, dancing and kicking out his rear legs.

Before Everett could calm him and regain control, the horse had skittered forward between Avarall and Wyot and on to the crossroads.

Arledge cried out a warning, but it was too late. Horse and rider had vanished.

Stillness descended on the woods. The birds returned to the trees, and an oppressive silence reigned.

Meryall turned to look at Arledge. He had fixed his gaze on the crossroads.

'We must follow and help Everett find his way home,' she said.

Arledge shook his head. 'I will go alone – you have had too recent an adventure of this nature, I cannot countenance you being placed in danger again.'

Meryall shook her head impatiently. She turned to Madoc. 'You, Wyot and Avarall must remain here to guard the path. Be vigilant and stay away from the centre of the paths.'

Madoc looked at her closely. Meryall's lips were drawn firmly together, her eyes hard.

'If you go, the party here will be unsupported if we encounter further magical interference… Why do you not stay and I will go with Arledge?'

Meryall hesitated. She had not considered this. Madoc raised his eyebrows. Looking sideways, he half caught Arledge's eye. Arledge frowned for a moment before his face cleared and he nodded discretely at Madoc.

'You must defend our friends here, Meryall. We cannot leave them without magical assistance. I surmise that the apothecary intended to delay us here and perhaps drive you into his trap. Therefore, we must resist and be ready,' he said.

Meryall took a long breath. 'If the apothecary is tracking us, it is better if you remain here to confront him,' she said meeting Arledge's eye squarely.

He paused for thought. Meryall stepped towards him and took his hands.

'There are no safe options, Arledge, we face risk at every turn. We must use our resources effectively. You are stronger than I in the ways of the cunning folk.'

Arledge inclined his head. 'There is wisdom in what you say, Meryall. Go, then, but remember that you must be respectful – you enter the realm of the goddess. Harm to any of those in her dominion will incur her wrath.'

He embraced her tightly. Releasing her, he smoothed her hair on her shoulder.

Avarall and Wyot raised their voices in agreement – it

was necessary to split the skills of their party, leaving an armed warrior and a magical defendant here and sending a magical practitioner and armed man after Everett.

Madoc smiled and tapped the short sword at his side. He rarely carried it, but Meryall knew that in his travels overseas, Madoc had been required to make use of it on many occasions and was by no means easy to overwhelm with force.

She looked at the crossroads ahead of them. Who knew what they would find on the other side of the sacred veil.

Chapter 19

Madoc and Meryall went forward on foot, not wanting to risk any ill consequence to their horses. They passed over the hawthorn path, boots touching the point in the road where generations of feet had trodden decades of berries into the ground. Meryall noticed little change as they crossed the threshold. Doubting at first whether they had traversed elsewhere, she looked back over her shoulder, half expecting to see the rest of the party waiting, but there was only empty space on the path behind her. They stood, regarding their new surroundings.

The pressure of the air felt subtly different, and the light had a golden tone that Meryall could not recall seeing on the other side of the path, but the forest around them appeared otherwise unchanged. She stepped forward and examined the path carefully, motioning to Madoc to join her. They stood together looking at the road ahead. The ground was relatively dry and firm, but they could trace the movements of Everett's horse. The tracks moved a little way across the hawthorn path, before Everett had turned his horse and continued onwards. Evidently, he had investigated the entry point to see if he could return to the others and concluding that he could not, had moved on along the path.

The path wound on through the trees. They proceeded with caution, observing the tracks closely and checking around them for signs of Everett – and for indications of danger in the unknown forest. Madoc kept his hand on his sword. They walked on and on. The place hummed with life. The sound of birds filled the air. Rays of light trickled between the branches, catching the flutter of butterflies amongst the flowers that studded the ground around the trees. Buttery yellow celandine stars shone brightly, next to the midnight velvet of sweet violet flowers. Meryall found the beauty of the woods seductive – without a mighty effort, one could forget that they were walking outside their own plane.

Meryall looked up at the sky. In the pale, crisp blue was the slender white crescent of the waning moon, already showing in the afternoon light. She could hear the tinkle of water nearby. Madoc stayed Meryall with a hand on her arm and pointed. A sudden movement in the trees caught her eye. Meryall made out the dappled coat of a deer. As their scent reached her, the doe looked up and skittered away through the forest, rousing three or four other does who had been grazing with her into a light-footed trot. They were soon out of sight. Meryall drew a breath.

In this other place, animals were sacred to those who held dominion over the land. She hoped that Everett had not been tempted to hunt, thinking himself lost without provisions.

The space around the path to the left opened up, and Everett's tracks wandered off the path and into the woods. Madoc crouched, scrutinising them, then motioned Meryall to continue.

The sound of the water drew closer. The trees cleared and they found themselves at the bank of a pool, with a burbling stream tumbling through the forest to pour into the clear waters. Madoc took a flask from his pouch and was about to advance towards the pool when Meryall cried out, rushing forward.

There, under the water, was Everett. His face was still as if in sleep, his hair drifting in a soft halo around his head in the stillness of the pool.

Madoc made to leap into the water, but Meryall stopped him, taking hold of his arm and crying out,

'Who is the patron of this pool?'

A shape emerged from amongst the trees. A grey-cloaked figure, small and slight, stepped towards them drawing back their hood. An old woman with white hair and dark, fathomless eyes regarded them.

'Who asks?' she said, her voice aloof and haughty.

Meryall bowed her head. She shivered. They were in the presence of the dark mother – the goddess in her aspect as crone, keeper of wisdom and guardian of the underworld. 'We are but travellers, Lady, seeking a friend who became lost in your realm. We've just found him in your pool and believe him to be dead.'

The woman looked shrewdly at them both. 'And how does a wanderer find themselves lost within a realm that is so secret?'

Madoc stepped forward. 'We believe that the hawthorn path was tampered with by a dark force, with the intention of causing harm to those on his trail.'

The woman frowned. 'Those travelling to this place are usually seekers of wisdom, knowledge or help. Your friend is imprisoned in my waters because he frightened my deer and sought to drink from the sacred pool. He did not appear to appreciate the sanctity of my realm.'

'Indeed, Lady, he found himself here unexpectedly and unwillingly, separated from the rest of his party. He had no understanding of nor wish to enter this place,' Meryall said.

The woman stepped away from them regarding Everett's form in the water. 'This is a highly unusual circumstance. I am concerned to hear that someone would misuse the sacred pathway so.'

Madoc moved to her elbow. 'The man we pursue has been involved in the misuse of the old magics in addition to evil deeds against his fellows. He is the son of a great cunning woman. However, it appears that although he has some of her knowledge, his spirit has twisted and darkened. We are unsure why he has committed acts of such destruction, but we pursue him to ensure that he cannot continue to cause harm.'

The woman looked at Madoc, taking in his strong, earnest features. She smiled. 'You are a good man. I see in you a kind heart. It is noble of you to try to rescue your friend.' She looked at them each in turn. 'You risked much in coming after him.'

Madoc drew Meryall to his side. 'My beloved is also a cunning woman. The man we seek has attempted to inflict grave harm upon her too, in order to evade detection.'

The woman clucked her tongue, her eyes scouring Meryall's face. 'Yes, I see the marks upon you still. You have been touched by a dark force, though your strength has kept you pure.' She sighed, turning back to the pool. 'Yet those who come here must pay the price of their passage back to their own world. It is the way of this place.'

Meryall raised her hands to her neck and began to unfasten her necklace. The woman uttered a deep laugh. Her back still to them, she raised her hand waving Meryall away.

'No, child, I do not seek gold. You must do better than that. I seek answers to my questions. If your answers please me, you may leave my realm.'

Madoc and Meryall looked at each other, eyes wide.

'Now, answer me this. What three things may no man know?'

Madoc furrowed his brow. Meryall thought hard, trying to formulate an answer.

'The pain of a woman?' she hazarded.

The lady shrugged. 'Go on. I will hear all three before I decide whether your answers please me.'

Meryall took a deep breath. 'Very well. The pain of a woman, the date of his death and the depth of his ignorance.'

The lady smiled, her eyes sparkling. 'Quite so, quite so. Now, my next question is for you,' she said, turning to Madoc. 'Tell me three things that no wise woman desires.'

Madoc rubbed his hands over his face, deep in thought. 'A wise woman wishes no weapon other than her tongue—' he started.

'I like not your answer. A wise woman understands she needs no weapon, her strength alone protects her. Try again.'

Madoc glanced at Meryall. She shrugged helplessly.

'No wise woman desires to be known to be wise, to be believed to be infallible and to have wisdom without experience,' Madoc said, his eyes creeping back to Everett's still, peaceful form under the water.

The woman inclined her head regally. 'Good, good. One more question then, for your free passage from my realm.' She turned back to Meryall. 'What three things does a mouse know that a lion does not?'

Meryall plucked nervously at her necklace, eyes raised to the sky as she thought.

'What does a mouse know that a lion does not?' she whispered to herself. She cleared her throat. 'The ways of the ants … the value of silence and…' She paused, uncertain. '…how the underside of the lion's chin looks?'

The lady tilted her head in thought, frowning at Meryall. Abruptly, the woman's face crumpled into a maze of lines, her eyes hidden in deep creases, and her chest heaved in huge, silent spasms. Madoc squeezed Meryall's hand urgently, trying to tug her away from the woman. Meryall stood transfixed, unsure of what to do. A breathy, wheezing sound reached her ears. She was laughing. The lady was laughing so hard that tears coursed down her cheeks.

Recovering herself, the lady chuckled, taking Meryall's face in her hands. Meryall felt a pulsing power at the touch of the gnarled fingers.

'I know that you have great wisdom and strength, my

child. Now go, take your companions and return to your own plane. I will watch over all of you – with interest.'

The woman stepped towards the water holding her hands wide before her. She raised them up to the sky, and as she did so, Everett's form emerged from under the water, dripping, silent and still.

Suspended in the air, Everett moved towards the bank, seemingly continuing to sleep. The unseen force directed by the woman's hands laid Everett gently on the ground.

Madoc stepped over to him and knelt beside him, stroking the hair from his face. He placed his ear close to Everett's nose to check whether he could hear breath in his body. Everett coughed, water streaming from his mouth.

Madoc supported him to a sitting position as he woke with a start. Meryall gave Madoc a smile of relief.

'Thank you, Lady,' Meryall said. 'You are generous and wise, and we thank you for allowing us safe passage from your realm.'

The lady turned away from them, gesturing towards the path. 'Go, my friends. You have an adversary to pursue.'

Meryall watched her move soundlessly into the trees. As the lady turned at the fork of the path, she saw a flash of dark hair under her hood and the edge of a smooth cheek. Meryall shook her head in wonder at the mysteries of the goddess.

Meryall and Madoc supported Everett to his feet. Everett appeared dazed but was recovering quickly. He was soon able to retrace his steps and locate his horse.

The companions returned to the path, and at the hawthorn path crossroads, their steps returned them to their realm.

Chapter 20

Arledge, Wyot and Avarall rushed forward, seeing their companions emerge suddenly upon the crossroads. Arledge smiled a welcome to all. Avarall gave Everett a rough hug, clapping him on the back with a smile of joy.

'We must continue,' said Meryall. 'We are under the protection of the lady of this place. I do not believe we need fear any further entrapment on this path.'

'The lady? You saw her?' said Arledge, wide-eyed.

Meryall smiled. 'Yes, our friend here,' she said gesturing to Everett, 'was most fortunate to escape eternal imprisonment in the waters of the lady's pool.'

After many questions to the wanderers and a drink from their flasks to restore their strength and will to go on, the party remounted and returned to the trail.

The fairy caves lay a few miles ahead of them yet. Meryall's confidence in their safety, while they continued in the woods, did not transfer to Avarall and Everett, who remained tense and alert, returning to their defensive riding formation.

Shortly after noon, the path opened to reveal a handsome stone manor, the residence of the sheriff and keeper of the forest. It was built of the local stone and sat half facing the woods, with the river falling away from the house at the rear.

The household had been watching for their arrival. A small figure emerged from the house and waved them to approach. They turned their horses towards the gates. The figure disappeared into the doorway, replaced by a tall, imposing man Wyot hailed as Sheriff Brian Cronshaw.

Brian came forward and greeted them. 'We have been keeping an eye on your man from a discreet distance,' he said, without preamble, but with a smile and wave incorporating them all in a cheerful welcome. 'As you said he would be, he is in the caves. Alone, as far as we can tell.'

Wyot clasped Brian's hand warmly. 'Thank you, Brian. It's good to see you – and still better to have your assistance.'

Brian waved away Wyot's thanks. 'You have done as much for me before and would likely do as much or more again.'

Brian turned his attention to the group at large. 'You will need to dismount – the path to the cave lies across the stepping stones over the river and into deep woods. We will take charge of your horses while you are gone. They will be well-rested and fed by the time you return.'

He looked up at the sky. 'It is likely that you will be unable to return home before dark – you are of course welcome to stay.'

Avarall stepped forward. 'We have had some difficulties with a trap laid along our path already … can you provide us with someone who knows the way to the caves well and can find us a path that the apothecary may not be expecting us to take?'

Brian bowed. 'I have briefed my best tracker to help you. She was born here and knows every tree and crag of those woods.'

Avarall smiled in satisfaction, the tension in her shoulders easing. 'Thank you, that will give us a decided advantage.'

Everett was making a rapid assessment of their surroundings and caught Avarall's eye to share his relief that they had a guide. The woods were thick and tangled; it would have been a challenge to move their group through the narrow, unknown paths without help.

They declined Brian's offer of refreshments and surrendered their horses to his care and their safety to a slim, active-looking girl of around fifteen years of age whom he introduced as Violet. Her confident steps led them across a series of stepping stones set into the broad river. Reaching the far side, they moved up the grassy bank and into the margins of the forest. The trees, beginning as a fringe of willow and alder, rose above the river, clothing the ridges and folds of a land carved out by ancient waters. The lie of the land soon became difficult to make out, as the trees grew more closely knit. Oak, ash and birch trees stood with branches intertwined and their roots radiating out like a web of veins across the forest floor, beneath a carpet of spring green.

Meryall, becoming acutely aware of the advantage such a landscape gave to an unseen enemy, began to share Avarall and Everett's fears. Her growing anxiety brought a sharpness to her senses – she could smell the musk of foxes, the old, dusty bark of ancient trees, and the scent of newly mown hay rose from the woodruff crushed by their passing feet. The trees had begun to come into leaf, closing down the range of their vision, as the foliage danced in the breeze and dappled sun all around them.

Meryall thought about the man they sought and the uncertainty of his future. She considered the small snatches of information they had gained about him – the harshness of his mother, the cunning woman; his seeming respectability in the town of Lune; the deceit and villainy of his conduct. She found it difficult to make out who the apothecary really was.

He appeared so loosely connected to other people, so superficially known by his community. What must have happened in this man's life to give him such powerful anger and bitterness towards others? And how and why did this connect to Eda and Lord De Lune? Could he really be a brother of Lord De Lune? But if so, why target Eda instead of Lord De Lune himself? She was puzzled, but she acknowledged that it was beyond doubt that he was adept and dangerous.

Her mother had taught her the cunning ways. Meryall had regretted many times over that she had lost her mother so young – the grief of this had cast a shadow over her life for a while, but the loss of her knowledge and skill as a teacher was a still more enduring loss. Meryall was under no illusions – she was skilful at charms and divination, but there were many deeper, more profound magics that her mother had never had the opportunity to share with her. Meryall glanced at Arledge, walking at her side. She had hoped that she would be able to spend some time with Arledge one summer, but her business had grown busy, her life with Madoc comfortable. Arledge was growing old. He might not be there to teach her if she continued to put off her studies. Sensing her glance, Arledge looked up and caught her eye with a smile. Meryall returned his smile and looked away, feeling guilty that her thoughts had wandered into a calculation of the imminence of his death.

Violet drew to a stop, raising her hand to halt the party. They had advanced to the lower slopes of a hill. The trees became sparser above them as the hill rose, a rocky outcrop visible to their right. She lifted her head and gave a piercing, high-pitched call, followed by three more, imitating a peregrine. They heard an answering call from high on the hill. Violet beckoned the group around her.

'The entrance to the caves lies within that outcrop,' she said, gesturing up the hill. 'My sister has been keeping watch above the entrance – her call back confirms that your man has not left the caves. We are not aware of another exit.'

They stood looking up the hill for a moment. The air was filled with a startling peregrine call once again. Violet frowned, scanning the land above her.

'He's coming out.' she said, her face intense. They crept forward, keeping close together in a tight knot. Advancing foot by foot, they drew near enough to make out a tall figure standing in front of an aperture in the rock.

'I know you are here!' Richard Mangnall's voice rang out, loud and clear, sending birds chattering from the trees near the cave.

Arledge and Wyot exchanged a glance. Arledge stepped forward, into the apothecary's line of sight. 'Greetings, Richard. My name is Arledge. We have something in common, I believe, you and I.'

Richard advanced a few steps, taking a long look at Arledge. 'I know who you are. My mother spoke of you.' His voice was scornful. 'She regarded you as skilled, which is all the more reason for me to dislike and distrust you. Get back, man, you know it is not you whom I wish to speak with.'

Arledge half turned to look back at the others, shrugging.

Madoc stepped forward. 'Talk to us, Richard. We can resolve nothing if you do not talk.'

The apothecary glanced at his counterpart and looked away. 'I have no quarrel with you, Madoc. It is your woman I would speak with.'

Madoc shook his head. 'I cannot say that I trust you to speak with her. You have tried to cause her harm.'

Richard's eyes flickered to the trees, where he could see the outline of the others.

'I regret that it was necessary to do so. I did not have a choice.'

Meryall frowned. She stepped forward, ignoring Madoc's restraining hand on her arm as she passed him. 'There is always a choice. Always another way,' she said, her voice rising in anger.

Richard laughed hollowly. 'It is the privilege of naivety

to believe so,' he replied, his face taut with bitterness and pain.

Meryall cautiously reached out with her essence to touch his. Sensing her, he raised his head, frowning. Meryall pulled back. It had been enough – she had felt a deep wound in this man's heart – a dark swirl of anger which covered a hard, cold core of fear within him.

'Where would you have us talk, Richard?' she said. She heard a chorus of hissed disapproval from behind her. Ignoring this, she stepped closer to the apothecary.

'Come down to the cave and talk. I promise to do you no harm. I will hand myself to your sheriff when we are done.'

Chapter 21

The cavern was deep; they passed down a long tunnel before emerging in a large round chamber, the limestone arching high overhead, with a slight hole in the rocks above them allowing the afternoon light to flood through. The air was cold and filled with the scent of damp stone.

Meryall thought that though this was so unlike her own cosy cave, this cave too had likely once been a home, or perhaps a place of worship. She looked around, seeking tool marks or carvings on the rock.

The local folk held that these caves were inhabited by the fae. Meryall could see why. The caves had a tense, humming power about them that she found disconcerting.

The apothecary crouched on the floor below the hole, gathering tinder to strike a spark into the branches he had laid. He succeeded in setting the small stack of wood alight, inside the circle of stones he had set out.

The firelight danced on the walls of the cave – Meryall could see two small spaces in the walls leading into additional chambers. The apothecary's face was bloodless, and there were deep shadows under his eyes. He indicated that they sit before the fire. Meryall took a position across from the apothecary, with the cave's exit to her back. His quick eye noted her choice, and he quirked an eyebrow in disdain.

'I gave you my word, Mistress Meryall,' he said.

Meryall flushed a little. 'You can understand my caution, given that you almost trapped me once and sought to trap me a second time.'

Richard laughed shortly. 'Indeed, but then I had promised nothing, now I have.'

Meryall settled her skirts and pulled her cloak around her, covering her hands in her lap. The deep cold of the cave, mingled with the chill of anxiety in the core of her stomach made her shiver. She fought to push away her fear and focus on the task at hand.

'How did you know this place?' Meryall asked, in a conversational tone.

Richard took a deep, sighing breath. 'My mother would take me on long journeys in the summer sometimes, to the ancient sacred places. This was one of them.'

'I have heard that she was an uncommonly skilled cunning woman,' Meryall said, observing his face as she spoke. A flash of darkness crossed his features.

'Yes. Yes, she was talented. She knew not only the ways of the light path, but also the ways of the shadow path, which is an almost forgotten knowledge now. And I have felt for myself the power of this shadow path.'

'It would appear that you, too, are skilled in the ways of the cunning folk.'

Richard examined her closely, alert for indications that she mocked him.

Satisfied, he gave a short bow of assent. 'I regret that it was necessary for you to feel the touch of darkness so directly. In other circumstances, I would have been honoured to have shared my knowledge with you as a peer.'

Meryall kept her face carefully neutral. 'I thank you and share your regret for the extremity we find ourselves in.'

Richard closed his eyes and put his head back, uttering a low laugh, before placing his head in his hands and massaging his temples.

'It has been a long day, Meryall. Will you join me in a cup of mead?'

Richard had reached to pull a leather bag to his side and was taking from it a bottle and cups. Meryall hesitated. Richard stilled, his back still to her. Meryall sensed the anger rolling from him in waves, a palpable field around him that she feared would crush her to the ground. The possible options available to her flitted through her mind.

'I have eaten nothing since breakfast, Richard, and fear that so strong a drink may cloud my thinking,' Meryall replied.

Richard's shoulders relaxed. 'Ah, if that is all, I have bread and cheese also. Am I not a good host!'

He took out provisions, laying them on a cloth spread upon a flat stone. 'For a moment, I feared that you continued to dishonour me by doubting my word.'

Meryall took a piece of bread. Richard sliced a portion of cheese with a sharply bladed knife and handed it to her. Meryall took it with thanks. The bread was of a rough, dry, coarse texture suitable for travelling. It sat heavily in her mouth.

He poured out mead for them both. With a sardonic twist of his mouth, he indicated that she choose her cup. Meryall picked up the cup nearest to her and carried it to her mouth, sipping the mead.

It was fiery and well-flavoured. She could detect nothing amiss in the flavour, although she doubted not that he had the skill to conceal the taste of poison if he so wished. He raised his cup in a toast to her, taking a long drink.

'It is a fine mead,' Meryall ventured, seeking to regain ground in the rapport that they had established.

'My mother's recipe, of course,' Richard replied.

Meryall ate her bread and cheese, savouring the space to think that the meal provided her. She thought of her friends waiting for her outside the cave.

They would be anxious and no doubt furious at her for taking this chance. Meryall felt a flicker of uncertainty. She had thought that talking with the apothecary offered the least risk to their group overall and offered the best chance for a peaceful resolution.

She began to wonder if she had again underestimated the man. She wished he would come to the point but did not want to risk incurring his anger by hurrying him.

Finishing her meal, she brushed the crumbs from her gown and took up her cup of mead from the hearthstone.

The heat of the fire had warmed the mead. She found the warmth of the cup on her hands comforting and rolled it between her palms, sipping the sweet, honey drink.

'I find mead most pleasant when warm,' she said, hoping to engage the apothecary in opening up and talking once again.

He shrugged. 'I have no preference. In summer, I enjoy it chilled, in winter, it is pleasant warm. Like all things, it has its seasons and I my whims.'

Meryall murmured her agreement.

'I see that you are uncertain of my temper and do not wish to ask me questions for fear of provoking me,' Richard said.

Meryall was startled by his sudden candour but composed her face carefully. She met his gaze steadily. 'I did not wish to appear discourteous. It is, after all, customary to take refreshments before coming to the business in hand, I believe.'

Richard smiled.

His face was not unpleasant, Meryall reflected. His skin was sallow and his features rather gaunt, but his smile gave a hint of the boy she could imagine him as. His eyes, however, were another matter – haunted and haunting in their darkness.

'Well, now we have observed the rites of civilised behaviour, you are free to ask me anything you wish to.'

Richard's words were careless, but his fingers tapped hard on the side of his cup.

Meryall could still sense the anger under the placid

surface of his features and wondered that she had not noticed it when she had met him before.

'Well, Master Apothecary, like all good tales, it is perhaps best told from the beginning,' she said lightly.

'And where would you consider the beginning to be, Mistress Meryall?' He answered her bantering style, but his voice had a brittle quality to it that made Meryall feel deeply uneasy.

'That, Richard, is for you to decide. We both know the ending of our tale as it is now, only you can say when it began.'

He sat back for a moment, his eyes searching the rock of the cave about them for an answer. Returning his focus to Meryall, he gave an ironic little bow. 'Like all such stories, it starts when I was a child.' He gave a dry laugh.

Meryall made her face neutral and acknowledged his statement by inclining her head and listening politely.

'My mother, Sitha Mangnall, as you know, was a cunning woman of great repute,' he said, his voice a scornful sing-song. 'However, you may not know that she was also a harsh and unforgiving woman, prone to anger and bitterness.'

Only the slightest spasm of his throat, constricting his voice for a moment, belied the emotion the apothecary felt.

'From my earliest memory, she told me that my father was dead and that he was a pitiful wastrel. It was many years, long after my mother's death, before my poor stepfather, on his deathbed, told me that she had lied to me. My father had been the late Lord De Lune – the current lord's father. They had formed a relationship, however, he, growing tired of her, had thrown her from him. Whether or not he knew that she was pregnant with his son, I cannot know with any certainty, but it is clear that my mother viewed me from my birth as a reproach and a reminder of her failed relationship. She was an angry, bitter woman.'

Meryall remained silent, experiencing a small measure of satisfaction that her surmise about his true father had been correct but was unsure about his statement about his mother not wanting him. Of all women, a cunning woman seemed the least likely to fall unintentionally pregnant or to continue with an unwanted pregnancy.

She wondered at Sitha's motives in falling pregnant. She remembered hearing that the late lord had been cruel and despotic. It had been an inauspicious start in life if what the apothecary said was true.

'But your mother must have been skilled with herbs—' she began cautiously.

Richard snorted. 'Yes, she was. She wanted a child when she fell pregnant. She thought that it would secure her a luxurious place in the castle with Lord De Lune, but when he repulsed her and declared that there were those amongst his men who would testify that the child was theirs and not his if he required them to do so, she was furious. By then, of course, it was too late for her to end her pregnancy without endangering her own life. And so I was born, the product of her scheming and a reminder of her failure.'

Meryall felt a kindling sense of sympathy for the man, unwanted and slighted from the moment he drew breath, the moment he came into the world as a fresh little soul, full of promise. Something of her thoughts must have shown on her face.

'I do not tell you this to seek sympathy, mistress,' Richard said with contempt in his tones. 'I merely tell you to explain my connection to the Lune family.'

'Then the present lord is your half-brother?' Meryall asked.

'Yes, not that he knows it.' Richard's mouth fleetingly contracted into a half- smile, half scowl.

'Why did you never make this known to him?' Meryall said.

Richard looked at her fiercely, as if trying to assess whether she was mocking him. 'What do you think he would say, mistress? Welcome to the family, here is half of my estate? He would never acknowledge me, and I have no proof now that my mother and stepfather, who appear to have been the only people to have known of my true parentage, are dead.'

Observing a muscle in the apothecary's jaw begin to jump as he clenched his teeth tightly, Meryall tried to find a less risky line of conversation.

'Did you get on well with your stepfather? You lived with him for some time after your mother's death?'

A deep sadness reached Meryall, pulsing from Richard's heart like blood from a wound.

'My stepfather was a good man and deserved better than my mother. The years I spent living with him after her death were the happiest of my life. He was a kind man, although unable to stand up to my mother.'

Meryall grieved for him – to have found a loving parent after his experiences, only to have that parent taken away seemed terribly unfair. She wondered if he would have reached the same excesses of bitterness and anger without this bereavement.

'I am sorry for your loss,' she said simply.

Richard hesitated, glaring as if he would make a bitter response, but accepted her words and was silent for a moment.

Meryall let the silence rest between them for a moment, before prompting him.

'You learnt the cunning ways from your mother?'

Richard sighed. 'Yes, she was a harsh teacher, but I cannot deny that she was knowledgeable. After her death, I renounced the cunning ways for some years, too angry and bitter about her treatment of me to want anything that reminded me of her. However, after my stepfather's death, after he told me … I started using the cunning ways to aid me in watching my half-brother, determined to see for myself the birthright I had lost.'

Meryall tried not to show her disapproval. In the same way that the apothecary's oath was to do no harm, the cunning folk had their customs, and it was frowned upon to use your skills for deception or covert observation with malicious intent. It was believed that to do so was to risk punishment and ill consequences from the gods. Richard did not look up at her but appeared aware of the course of her thoughts.

'I am in no need of a lecture on the code of the cunning folk, Mistress Meryall. As you see, I am experiencing the consequences without the assistance of your notice.'

'I have found Lord De Lune reasonable. Did you consider approaching him to explain your situation?' Meryall asked.

Richard's eyes blazed. 'Reasonable? Yes, I suppose he is. Even if he had not believed me, most likely he would have done what he did with Eda and his other women and attempted to pay me off. He would have set me up somewhere far away where I would not endanger his attempts to woo a Christian bride with what her family would see as the shame of a rumoured illegitimate brother.'

Meryall thought about this and had to acknowledge a degree of justice in his words. It was not their custom to differentiate between births from within marriage and births without. Lord De Lune, however, she could see, valued his aspirations above tradition. Although he would have attempted to make amends, as Richard said, this would have been through monetary repayment, which would not truly repay Richard what he had lost in social standing and kinship. If he had sought support from the law, the lack of living witnesses would have weakened Richard's case significantly.

'I hoped in time—' Richard hesitated. 'I hoped in time that I would become indispensable to him. That when he found out what I had done to safeguard his interests, he would accept me … if I could not prove my blood connection, I could still prove my worth to him.'

Meryall was silent for a long moment. Richard's behaviour was a bizarre mirror to Lord De Lune's own – but with a lack of control and a sinisterness that was difficult to fathom. Lord De Lune too had been subjected to a challenging childhood, but despite his ruthless reputation as a trader did not appear to indulge in this level of wrongdoing. What made the difference? The sheltering effect of the privilege of rank? Disposition? It was impossible to know.

'You were watching Eda, too?' Meryall asked eventually.

The apothecary's face softened. 'Yes. Poor Eda. She is a clever woman – a good match for Lord De Lune. If he had just married her, none of this would have been necessary.'

'You found out she was pregnant by chance, through Aelcea Allred?' Meryall pressed.

Richard looked down at his hands, spreading his long fingers and knitting them together tightly. 'I could not let her tell anyone,' he said quietly.

'Why?'

Richard looked up at Meryall.

'Because Eda would suffer – she had promised not to tell anyone of her relationship with him. If Aelcea guessed at the father, Eda would lose her settlement, and Lord De Lune may have lost his German bride. My usefulness to him would have been destroyed.'

Meryall was silent. She did not wish to provoke Richard – he may shut down and stop talking if she shamed him. It took much strength not to laugh in derision at the notion of the apothecary trying to prevent Eda from suffering, after all he had done.

'I can see that you cared about Eda. What did you do to take care of her?' Meryall asked.

Richard appeared disarmed by her gentle tone and her apparent acquiescence.

'I care about Eda. When I found she was with child...' His eyes were fixed on the fire and he looked beyond it, lost in thought.

Meryall's movement, as she replaced her mug on the stone, roused him from his reverie.

'I could not let her and her child suffer what I have suffered – to be cut off from the society, and the wealth and consequence that should belong to them. I could not let her child be subject to the shame and loneliness I have experienced.'

His words came quick and low. They hung in the air between them, heavy and filled with a lingering pain. Meryall could sense his pain, like a thorn in the foot of a lion. As with a wounded lion, she knew that it was dangerous to advance too close to Richard. Her anger faded as she saw beneath the mask of the adult man. Before her, in the depth of his eyes, she saw a frightened child who knew no other way of keeping himself safe than to try to control the world around him by any means necessary.

She sighed in sadness and frustration. The cruelty of a parent too often laid waste to more than just the life of the child. Her sympathy for him evaporated as she considered his behaviour – his wish to be of use to Lord De Lune and to inveigle himself into the position that fate had denied him appeared to her a more realistic motive than an attempt to shield an unborn child from a poverty and ignominy that was by no means certain. Was he trying to manipulate her, she wondered.

Meryall felt his mood change, his shame abruptly transforming into anger. His rage shimmered in the air between them.

'And then you found out about her, and I had to try to stop her talking. You were too close to the truth, too close to working it out. I could not reach Aelcea to prevent her telling you about Eda after your interfering apothecary cured her. That left me no choice but to silence Eda before you spoke to her and pieced it all together.'

He gazed at her, his carefully controlled hatred making his eyes cold and his features tight.

'It was your fault,' he hissed.

Meryall took a deep breath, centring herself and focusing on the shield of protection she cast around her. The apothecary's fury was intrusive, it pushed against her, grey hooks of dread snagging against her as he threw his energy at her.

'Don't,' Meryall said firmly.

Richard continued to focus on her for a moment, his presence crushing her, but then looked away, his anger subsiding. He put his head in his hands.

'I'm sorry,' he whispered.

Meryall took the opportunity of the moment.

'I don't understand why you killed Eda's brother, Avery,' she said.

Richard's face contorted, his eyes filling with tears. 'I

followed him for some days after he came to Lune looking for Eda. I confronted him in the woods. I told him about Eda's relationship with Lord De Lune and her establishment, offered him money to go away, but he wouldn't listen…'

'Wouldn't listen to what?' Meryall asked.

'I asked him to take my money, go to Eda, live with her and to stay away from Lune, but he became angry and impatient, determined to go back to the village and confront Lord De Lune. I could not let him do that; such public accusations! All would have been lost.'

Meryall swallowed back words of condemnation. It was a meaningless death.

Avery died merely because a slighted, troubled man-boy had wanted to win a place at the side of a brother lost to him by circumstance.

Eda's child, his own niece or nephew, had died because – and Meryall did not believe Richard's statement that he wished to spare the child his own fate – he feared that its birth and Aelcea's knowledge of it might endanger his plans to make himself indispensable to his brother. And Eda had nearly died merely because he had made such a mess of trying to do so.

She wondered what he had he expected Lord De Lune to say when he told him all that he had done to protect his prospects. Richard had misjudged his brother if he expected to be welcomed to a place by his side after all of his misdeeds in his brother's name.

Perhaps Richard had hoped to fall back on blackmail if

protestations of loyalty and devotion failed, she thought. Although again – she felt he had not understood his brother's nature if he expected Lord De Lune to be easily cowed by threats of exposure.

'Well, what next, Richard?' Meryall asked. 'It seems that you have told all there is to tell.'

The apothecary looked tired and deflated. 'I am ready to come with you. I cannot live with running forever. It would be easy to evade capture – I could leave you now if I used charms and a glamour upon you, but I want to face what I have done.'

There was relief on his face at having told the truth, that the path which had spiralled so far out of his control had ended.

Meryall smiled. 'That reminds me, your trick on the hawthorn path displeased the goddess greatly. I think you would be wise to make offerings to try to appease her.'

Richard sighed, returning her smile. 'I will remember that, although I deserve whatever vengeance she sees fit to bestow on me.'

'Are you ready?' Meryall asked.

Richard shook his head. 'Can we drink a final cup of mead before we go?'

Meryall assented. Richard poured her mead, handing the cup across the fire to her. He took up the bottle of mead and made to pour his own cup. Meryall's eyes darted to his hand. The apothecary was slipping a tiny vial into his sleeve. She put her own cup down untasted.

'What have you done?' she said coldly.

Richard closed his eyes, placing his fist against his mouth. Meryall rose and took his cup.

'Did you poison your own cup too, or just mine?' She stood over him, hands trembling with anger. She put the cups down out of reach.

'I did not poison your cup…' Richard whispered, '…only mine.' He raised his eyes to her face. 'You have to understand. I must punish myself, I must make amends, I–'

'Coward,' Meryall spat. 'You wished to take the easy way out. If you wish to make amends, then live. Learn to be a better person. Use your talents for good. Do not pretend that you wished to die for the sake of others.'

Richard sat frozen, his eyes fixed on Meryall's face.

'Give me the vial,' she said.

He took it from his sleeve, placing it in her hand obediently.

Meryall put it into the pouch at her waist. She looked down at him. He seemed shrunken, his arms wrapped around himself. Sighing, she picked up the cups, taking them to the far side of the cave.

'Do you have a water skin?' she asked.

He nodded, handing it to her. Meryall emptied the cups and swilled them out twice with water, refilling them with mead from the apothecary's flask.

She handed him a cup. 'Your mead.'

'Thank you.' His voice cracked with emotion.

They drank in silence.

'Do you favour dragon's claw or wormwood for divination?' Meryall asked, at last, seeking to calm him by talking about familiar matters.

'W-wormwood,' he said, 'but I value dragon's claw for dream walking.' His voice grew stronger as he spoke.

They sat and drank together, sharing talk of herbs, charms and books. Meryall had the sense that if he had been amongst cunning folk better able to guide him and provide him with a sense of kinship, they might not have arrived at where they were.

She thought once more about the nature of the man. No man, she thought, was irredeemable and Richard had gifts many people were not blessed with – intelligence, talent and, although sadly warped, the capacity for warmth and love, as evidenced by his regard for his stepfather. The seeds of his actions could not be unsown, however, and now Richard must reap his crop.

Chapter 22

They emerged blinking into the sun. Everett, Avarall and Violet had drawn bows trained upon the apothecary. Meryall put her hand on Richard's shoulder, giving it a squeeze of reassurance, then raised her hand and waved to her companions. They looked relieved, but their hands remained upon their weapons.

Richard shrugged. 'I cannot blame them.'

They walked down the slope together. Violet handed Everett a length of rope she had carried wrapped around her waist. Avarall held Richard's arms, while Everett bound his hands. In recognition of the rough terrain they had to cross on their journey back to the manor, his hands were tied in front of him, to allow him to catch himself if he were to fall.

The party were silent and pensive as they retraced their path through the forest. Meryall considered the future of this man who had let his past be the decider of his fate. As the crimes had happened to victims who resided in Lord De Lune's territory, it was his right to summon the court to try Richard. She could not think of the possible outcomes without pain, despite the seriousness of Richard's crimes. He would lose his livelihood, his liberty and although it was rare, there was the potential that he could lose his life if the court deemed him so dangerous that they considered that there was no alternative. There was also the price he would have to pay to the goddess for his misuse of the hawthorn path, which was perhaps still more formidable than the justice of men. Those who had committed transgressions against the goddess had seen for themselves her aspect as mistress of the underworld – commanding wraiths and fiends who could torment a soul beyond endurance.

The forest was cool and peaceful as they walked on, untroubled by the doings of the men and women who passed beneath the mighty canopy.

They reached the stepping stones more quickly than Meryall had anticipated and were soon on the far bank of the river and passing into the manor gate. Brian and his men had long since sighted them and awaited them, weapons drawn, in case they had need of assistance. Seeing their prisoner bound and compliant, Brian indicated that they stand down. He came forward and shook Wyot's hand heartily. Wyot ordered that a basement chamber be readied to contain the apothecary. Meryall frowned. Catching her eye, Wyot added that the man would need a hot meal, water to wash and drink and a decent blanket. Brian waved his assent and at his signal, his men moved off to make the preparations.

Brian invited them all within, assigning them chambers and promising that hot water and refreshments would be brought to them as soon as possible. They retired gratefully to their rooms. Meryall and Madoc's room was spacious and comfortable, with a large, plump bed and crisp linen. A pair of straight-backed chairs sat to either side of the fireplace. Meryall was thankful for the fire. The chill of exhaustion and overtaxed energy filled her stomach, making her teeth chatter. She felt Madoc's eyes on her back but continued to warm her hands at the flames.

'You need not tell me of the dangers of my actions, Madoc. I am fully aware.'

Madoc shook his head in frustration. 'That may rather worsen the situation. If you were ignorant of the extent of your rashness, it might be more readily forgivable.'

Meryall turned from the fire, the light catching her eyes. 'Forgivable? To whom do I answer? Whose forgiveness would be required had my refusal to talk with Richard ended in him being shot down by our people?'

'That is unfair, Meryall. You could have talked to us, agreed a plan, agreed a signal to let us know if you needed help. To simply proceed into the cave with him with no discussion was hasty and could have placed more than yourself in danger.'

The cold shaking in the pit of her stomach which had begun in fatigue now turned from ice to fire. Meryall blazed with anger.

'And you, Wyot and Arledge would not have tried to prevent me going?'

'What love would we have for you if we had not?' Madoc shot back.

Meryall rose swiftly to her feet, striding across the room and on down the stairs, eager to prevent the flow of words which she knew could not be unsaid. She found an outer door and walked out into the cool air. The stepping stones were away to her right. Drawn by the clean scent of the swiftly flowing water, Meryall jumped out onto the first step. The water flowed all around the little island at her feet and its movement gave her a moment of peace.

Skipping from stone to stone across the river and into the woods, she went onwards, seeking solitude. She had walked more than two miles when a tall oak with two mighty arms offered a fork into which she scrambled, finding a comfortable and secluded seat in its embrace. Meryall closed her eyes, focusing on her breath and feeling the tension in her body. Her muscles were tight and her system filled with the buzzing aftermath of stress. She allowed the stillness of the tree to touch her. The leaves whispered in the breeze. Meryall stiffened.

'Meryall.'

Undoubtedly, her name sounded in the whispering around her.

'Yes?' Her reply was scarcely more than thought.

'Only my body can be bound, my mind cannot be,' came the answer.

She saw the apothecary's form materialise before her, solidifying for a moment, seated on the branch beside her. smiling wryly before he vanished once more.

The air stilled around her for a moment, then she felt that she was once again alone. Meryall sat for a long time considering the visitation, and its implications. She found herself torn between taking comfort in the notion of Richard retaining some freedom – she found the prospect of incarceration as a punishment hard to countenance – and fear of his dangerousness. Unless imprisoned in isolation, well away from people, was there any safety for herself and others? A dark afterthought added itself – is there any safety while he lives? Meryall was unsettled and ashamed of this thought, for she believed it to be barbaric to kill people for their crimes.

The tree had left green mossy smudges on the fabric of her skirt when she climbed down. Meryall dusted off her skirts as she walked back through the golden late- afternoon light. Her knowledge of Madoc – and his of her – was such that both knew when it was sensible to take time away from one another and that the time to talk would arrive again when the immediacy of their feelings had cooled and made space for thought. She had no doubt that they would both benefit from this respite from each other but found her thoughts turning with increasing concern to the journey ahead of them all and the implications of the journey's end for Richard.

The others had assembled in a large room with handsome wood panelling. The panels, sturdy tables and chairs – wrought of oak from the Forest of Bowland – all shone with the patina of regular dusting and polishing, and Meryall could detect the faint scent of beeswax polish. She took a seat next to Madoc, squeezing his knee under the table. He pushed his knee against hers in greeting and smiled. Wyot and Brian were deep in conversation with Avarall and Everett about the logistics of transporting the apothecary to Lune. Meryall's skin chilled as she remembered the whispered message she had received in the woods. Meryall could walk from her body when needed – dreamwalking was a form of this, but she could only make herself known to others who slept. Meryall knew of few cunning folk who could communicate with people in the waking world – Arledge being the only one known to her personally. Even Arledge could only do this over short distances. She sighed inwardly. She must ask Arledge about it. It was also time to speak to Arledge about agreeing on a date to start a period of study with him. Meryall felt a keen desire for the knowledge she knew she must gain, but a wariness at the changes this would bring to her life. Much as she had hungered for freedom, now that there was a prospect for some newness and excitement, she found herself feeling reluctant to leave the comforts of her cottage and the familiarity of the village's quiet, regular routines.

'I will send two of my people with you so that you have sufficient bodies to be able to have a rear guard, and riders ahead and to each side of the prisoner,' Brian said.

Wyot gave his agreement and thanks. Meryall listened with interest to their plans. If they set off early, it would be possible to reach Lune in a day's ride, which was preferable to breaking their journey and staying a night on the road with a captive – especially a captive who could leave his body at will.

'I will make sure that your people receive a good meal

and a snug night's lodgings before they return to you,' he assured him.

Meryall prayed that the goddess would watch over them on their return to Lune. Their recent journeys had been far too eventful.

Chapter 23

Meryall and Arledge sat on a fallen tree trunk overlooking the river, watching a heron pick its way through the shallows on its elegant long legs. The others had not yet risen. Arledge was deep in thought – Meryall felt that his eyes looked beyond the river bird he seemed to regard. She had been anxious about telling him about Richard's visit to her. Meryall knew Arledge to be a just man, but her news may compel him to advise that Richard should be executed rather than imprisoned. She was beginning to get a sense of an alternative – but she needed Arledge to explain to her how Richard had been able to visit her, and to speak to an old friend in Lune before she was confident to put forward her idea. Meryall hoped that Arledge would contain his views about Richard's risk and the measures needed to manage it until they met with Lord De Lune. By that time, she would established whether her idea was possible.

Meryall gave a calm, considered description of the apothecary's visit to her. Arledge's face became increasingly serious as he listened.

He sighed, steepling his fingers in front of him. 'I am not surprised. Sitha Mangnall too was talented in travelling beyond her body. These skills are often in the blood. Even so, there are few cunning folk left who are strong travellers.'

'Aside from yourself, of course,' Meryall said to him with a fond smile.

Arledge shook his head with a laugh. 'There are far more skilful travellers than I.'

He returned his gaze to the heron, still picking through the shallows, in search of fish.

'Is physical proximity necessary for Richard to reach out to a person as he did?' Meryall asked Arledge, breaking through his reverie.

Arledge thought for a long moment before answering. 'It has been many years since I have encountered someone who is proficient in this skill. I have practised it over short distances but have not ventured more than a mile and a half since I was a young man. It takes much energy.'

Realising that he had not answered her question, Arledge laid an apologetic hand on Meryall's arm.

'It is possible to visit places some distance from where your physical body resides, but it takes considerable effort, and the proximity affects the extent of your power. At a close range, a person may exert magical influence. At a distance of more than two miles, even the strongest amongst us could only make our voice heard, and our presence felt, at best.'

Meryall nodded thoughtfully. She had been above two miles away from Richard when he had appeared to her, yet she had both heard his voice and seen him, in addition to sensing his presence. He was undeniably a skilful traveller.

'Are there any conditions that confound a person's attempts to send out their presence in this way?' she asked.

Arledge looked at her shrewdly. 'It is troublesome to attempt to travel across the sea – it can be done, but it limits the power of one's projections to voice alone.'

Meryall hid her interest carefully and moved the conversation to the other matter she knew she must raise with Arledge – the plans for the commencement of her apprenticeship.

The others were at the table in the great hall breaking their fast when they returned. Arledge was in particularly good spirits and sat down to talk and eat with enthusiasm. Wyot, Brian and the armed guards sat at the other end of the table, earnestly rehearsing their stratagems, procedures and shifts. Meryall caught Avarall's eye for a moment and smiled. Avarall's face was serious, but her cheeks held a flush of excitement at the importance of their mission.

All was packed, the sturdy horses loaded and all but the guards mounted when Richard was brought out into the courtyard, squinting against the sudden brightness of the day. His wrists were bound before him, and Avarall and Everett seated him on a horse, binding him to the saddle to prevent him falling and to discourage attempts to dismount. Meryall looked at Richard, seeking his eye, but he did not meet her gaze.

Their early start meant that they made good progress. The party stopped for food and to water the horses an hour or so before noon and reached the outskirts of Lune in the early afternoon. Brian had sent a messenger ahead the previous day, and they were greeted at the town walls by a knot of Lord De Lune's guards, who had been instructed to accompany them to the castle.

Lord De Lune awaited them in the courtyard of the castle. His men untied Richard from his saddle and roughly marched him through the gates, heading towards the stone dungeons beneath the towers. Lord De Lune's face was filled with dark anger as he watched the guards walk the apothecary away. Richard's eyes remained cast towards the ground. Recollecting himself, Lord De Lune turned with a smile and shook the hands of Wyot, Brian and the guards, before kissing Meryall's hand, greeting Madoc and introducing himself to Arledge. He summoned a servant to take them within, assign them quarters and see to their needs. They arranged to meet again at the evening meal, which Lord De Lune had instructed was to be served in the intimacy and privacy of his quarters.

Meryall called for water to wash and sat down with Madoc to eat of the arrangement of dried fruit and cheeses placed in their quarters and to drink a long draught of cool ale while they waited.

The dust of the road sat heavily in her nose and mouth, and she felt sore and fatigued by the journey. She had seldom ridden on horseback in recent years, yet her investigations in this matter had obliged her to ride long distances, and her muscles were seeking to remind her of this.

Madoc was unpacking herbs to brew to ease their muscles. She traced with pleasure the scent of meadowsweet, sage and hyssop. Although in years gone by, Madoc had travelled widely, across land and sea, it had been a long time since he had ridden so much and he too was sore. Meryall felt a rush of affection watching his strong hands and handsome, kind face as he worked.

They had spent many years together, yet Meryall was troubled at times by her reserve and lack of openness with Madoc. He accepted this without question and mostly without censure, but Meryall knew her guardedness was unnecessary and unfair.

She cast her mind back over her life. Since her father's death when she was a child, Meryall thought, she had been much more reserved, even with her mother. She regretted that too and reminded herself that she must learn the lesson that loss had taught her – tomorrow was not always vouchsafed, she should share what she needed to say today. She would tell Madoc of her conversation with Arledge and their plans for her apprenticeship when they returned home, but first, she must confide in him her intention to plead on Richard's behalf.

There was a knock at the door, and the servant entered with water, pushing this idea from her mind for the moment. She would ask Madoc to come with her when she went to visit her old friend Carwyn and would tell him all on the walk to Carwyn's house. Carwyn had lived with Meryall and her mother for a few months when Meryall was a girl and Carwyn a young scholar. He had been travelling from his homeland of Wales when he had been taken ill. Unable to go any further, he had stayed with them until he recovered. Meryall and Carwyn had become good friends. She had tried to keep track of his progress in the world – he had reached the University of York on leaving them and had prospered in his studies. On completing them, he had gone to the sacred island of Bardsey for a while, to work as a scholar in the remote community, producing beautiful works of knowledge. He had been tempted back to Albion by the dean of the University of York, who had offered to support him in establishing a scholarship programme. The growing prominence of the schools in Albion had meant that there was an ever-increasing need for those who could add to the works of the extensive libraries, which were the wonder of the civilised world.

The afternoon was fading to gold as they stepped out of the castle and walked down into the town. Deep in conversation, the walk seemed short, though Carwyn's home was on the edge of Lune. They found themselves at the door of a large, stone-built house, with an ornately carved entrance. Meryall rapped on the door. They heard hurrying footsteps in the distance, the slapping sound of leather sandals hitting the flagstones. A slightly built young man, with a pale, grave face set with watery grey eyes, opened the door.

Meryall smiled. 'Blessings to you. We come to speak to Carwyn. My name is Meryall. This is my companion, Madoc.'

The young man looked doubtful and appeared about to ask them to wait outside when they heard a deep voice from within the house.

'Meryall? Can it truly be you?'

A tall man, some years older than Meryall, came forward, clasping the shoulders of the young man at the door.

'Please make ready some refreshments, Alun!'

Carwyn sent the young man on his way and swept Meryall and Madoc into the house in an easy manner. He grasped Meryall's hands and then enclosed her in a rib-creaking embrace.

'My, it is good to see you!'

Madoc looked mildly surprised at Carwyn's enthusiastic greeting. Carwyn turned to Madoc on being introduced to him and grasped his hand, pumping it, before pulling him into a hearty hug. Madoc smiled and laughed rather awkwardly.

Steering them both to chairs within a huge recessed fireplace, Carwyn sat down and looked expectantly at Meryall.

'Well, tell me, what brings you here, my dear?'

'I had heard that since you had returned to Lancashire from Bardsey, you had established your house here, for graduates of York. I gather that you prepare them for scholarship at Bardsey and other places?'

'Yes, indeed, my scholars go on to work at many of the institutions that produce the finest books and manuscripts for our universities.'

Meryall bowed her head. 'My old friend, I have need of your advice.'

Chapter 24

The morning brought sunshine and the scent of green things coming to life. Spring was gathering pace, the soil was warming and fully awakening from its winter slumber, and buds unfurled upon the trees. Meryall awoke early. She had slept fitfully, her anxiety about Richard Mangnall's hearing making incursions into her dreams, which were filled with a lethargic dread. Madoc, having heard her proposal, finalised with Carwyn's advice, had reluctantly agreed to support her. His sense of justice demanded this of him, Meryall knew, despite his concern about the apothecary's dangerousness. She hoped that Lord De Lune would be open to her suggestion. It occurred to her that Richard may perceive her solution as more of a punishment than incarceration. She hoped not but had been too wary of him to seek him out through dream walking. Meryall was relieved, given their proximity within the castle, that he had not sought to reach out to her either. When she looked within her soul, she found her thoughts and feelings about the man to be deeply conflicted. It was wrong to kill another person as punishment for ending another person's life – this was a cycle of violence that did nothing to address the reasons why such crimes occurred, she was sure of that … and yet, he was a dangerous man. But would he always be a dangerous man? Could people make amends for such serious crimes? She hoped so – and would argue so with all her heart today.

Heavily carved panels of dark wood covered the walls of the castle's courtroom. The public gallery was tightly packed with jeering and stamping townsfolk. In the centre of the room, on a raised dais, were an enclosed box for the accused and the high-backed seats of the judging panel. Madoc, Meryall, Arledge, Avarall and Everett were given seats on the first bench in front of the dais. Wyot, Lord De Lune and an adviser Meryall had not previously seen sat on the grand chairs of the dais. Looking around, Meryall saw Carwyn at the front of the upper gallery. She smiled up at him, cheered by his broad, ruddy face.

Dishevelled and grey-faced, Richard was led into the room from a passage which allowed prisoners to be brought up from the dungeons. The crowd stamped and spat insults with increasing viciousness until the court usher banged loudly on the stone flags with his staff, calling for order.

Meryall caught a glimpse of Aelcea and Faron in the gallery and wondered whether her proposal would anger them. Nevertheless, it was her moral duty to propose a humane solution. Execution would not repair the wrongs the apothecary had done.

Lord De Lune had been hospitable and garrulous at

dinner the previous night, raising many toasts to them all for capturing the apothecary. Meryall sensed in him cold anger and resentment at his attempts to harm Eda, although he concealed this well. His face, as he sat on the dais, was impassive, his handsome features neutral and unmoved.

Lord De Lune stood and introduced the panel – the unknown advocate was Roger Newell – the magisterial assistant to Lord De Lune. His eyes burned in his pale face, and his fleshy mouth had an unpleasant, unwholesome look that made Meryall shiver.

Roger stood and read the charges against Richard – murder, administering poison with intent to harm and assault. His voice rang on the high stone ceiling of the courtroom, and there were murmurs from the assembled witnesses. The castle guards had limited the numbers of people who had been allowed to enter the room, but the twenty or so people gathered on the public benches sounded hostile and hungry for Richard's punishment. The guards who flanked Richard pulled him to his feet.

'How do you plead to these charges?' Roger demanded.

'Guilty,' Richard said, simply and quietly.

Lord De Lune turned to Wyot. 'My Lord Sheriff, do you wish to present your evidence to assist the court in sentencing?'

Wyot stood. He gave an unembellished, factual account of the evidence he had pieced together from their discussions and his own experience of Richard. Unemotional as his words were, the crowd on the benches hissed and muttered their disdain and hatred for Richard and his deeds.

Wyot finished giving evidence and returned to his seat.

Roger drew the proceedings to a close. 'Do you have anything you wish to say in your defence?' he asked Richard.

Richard looked out at the crowd, catching Meryall's eye. 'Only that I am sorry.'

Someone at the back of the gallery hurled an apple at him. It fell short of the mark and landed at his feet, the brown flesh of the rotten fruit smashed on the stone. It filled the stale air with the scent of cider.

Roger looked down at the apple, smirking. 'Then we adjourn to consider your punishment.'

The guards tugged Richard out of the stand, pulling harshly at his fetters and causing him to stumble and fall to his knees for a moment, to jeers from the crowd, as they disappeared back down towards the dungeons.

Lord De Lune stood and led the panel off the dais into the rooms behind, signalling to the guards to allow Meryall and their group to join them. Shouts of 'hang him!' rang out from the stalls.

The room behind the dais was still. The taint of old dust seemed to rise from the flagstone floor and hang in a blanket of silence. Benches ringed the walls of the small chamber. They took seats along two sides. Meryall sat next to Madoc, across from Lord De Lune.

Roger stood and began pacing the floor. 'It is clear that the people expect justice, My Lord. There is no option other than execution in this case.'

Meryall frowned. 'It is clear the people expect justice, sir, but it does not follow that execution represents justice.'

Lord De Lune smiled tiredly. 'Well, I am open to discussions, but my instinct would be to execute the man. Leaving aside the expectations of the people, how else may we manage his risk to the safety of others?'

'I have an alternative proposal,' Meryall began.

Roger stared at her. His eyes held a fanatical light but behind that,

Meryall detected ambition. It was not just that he believed fervently in punishment – he wanted to use this situation as an opportunity to raise his profile and popularity within the town and to demonstrate his usefulness to his lord.

Meryall shook her head almost imperceptibly as she thought how similar his motivation was to that of the man he sought to execute. He was not disposed to allow Meryall to prevent him from doing so.

'My Lord, I am sure that you are aware that Mistress Meryall–' Roger inclined his head in a pantomime of respectfulness '–has no authority in the matter of sentencing.'

'Thank you, Newell. I am, however, interested to hear her proposal.'

Lord De Lune's voice was smooth but carried an edge which prevented Roger from replying.

Meryall cleared her throat. 'I have consulted with a friend of mine – Carwyn ap Rhys. I believe he is known to you, Lord?'

'Yes, mistress – he is a fine scholar and an asset to the town. His establishment brings many visitors and students to Lune.'

Meryall nodded in agreement. 'As you may be aware,

Richard Mangnall is an exceptional scholar of herb lore and the ways of the cunning folk.'

'I cannot see how this is in any way relevant to his guilt,' Roger interrupted, his voice clipped and taut.

Lord De Lune tapped his fingers on the bench impatiently. 'Please continue,' he urged, ignoring Roger's look of disapproval.

'I would suggest that Richard's punishment be his banishment to the community of Bardsey,' Meryall said.

Lord De Lune raised his eyebrows. 'Many scholars would consider it a privilege to be allowed to live and work within the community of Bardsey – the sacred isle is renowned for its art, literature and advanced learning. I fail to see how it can be considered a punishment.'

Roger gave a smirk, satisfied with the reply of his lord.

'Carwyn assures me that there is a house on the island where Richard could reside – under the supervision of a powerful, cunning man. It is set apart from other dwellings, in an elevated part of the north-east of the island. Furthermore, Master Arledge will confirm that Richard's powers will be constrained by his distance from others and the barrier of the sea.'

Lord De Lune looked unconvinced.

Meryall pressed on. 'Regarding punishment – the removal of his status, rights and privilege are sufficient, I believe. Relieve him of the ownership of his shop and use the proceeds to pay reparations to his victims. Richard may also repay his community by producing works of scholarship which will benefit many others.'

'This is a woman's solution!' Roger cried, unable to contain himself. 'A soft, weak solution to the problem. What – this murderous wretch is to live a life which is more comfortable than that of many innocent, poor people? It cannot be! *Commodum ex iniuria sua nemo habere debet* – no wrongdoer should gain advantage from his wrong!'

'Ah, Master Roger,' Madoc said mildly, 'I see that you are in agreement with the words of Ferdinand of Germany – *fiat justitia, pereat mundus* – justice must prevail even if the world must perish over it. Our man must die to serve justice, though the world might receive greater reparation through him remaining alive.'

Roger grimaced and turned away. Meryall looked around. Arledge appeared uncertain, Wyot frowned, and Avarall and Everett refused to meet her gaze.

Lord De Lune rose to his feet and walked to the doorway, peering out at the crowd in the courtroom.

'The people would not understand such a nuanced decision,' he said.

'They will understand money however, Lord. They will understand that he will be made to work to pay compensation to his victims and that he will be stripped of his property and rights until he has repaid his wrongs and can be proven to pose no risk to others – if that ever can be proven.' Meryall clenched her jaw tightly, her hands white-knuckled in her lap as she sought to convince him.

'What if he refuses to comply?' Lord De Lune asked.

'Well, in that case, you will be able to consider the alternatives,' Meryall replied.

Lord De Lune motioned to a guard. 'Please bring me Carwyn ap Rhys and Richard Mangnall.'

Roger's face grew pale with anger, but he did not seek to interfere further.

Carwyn entered first. He waved a greeting to Meryall and Madoc and smiled at the others, before sweeping a half bow to Lord De Lune. He took a seat in an empty spot on the bench next to Avarall. Richard came into the room before his guards. They steered him ahead of them, his hands and feet shackled, brow knotted with confusion. He looked at the assembled faces and his eyes lingered on Carwyn, brow wrinkled in puzzlement.

Lord De Lune resumed his seat. 'Carwyn ap Rhys does us the honour of helping us to consider your fate,' he said to Richard. 'Mistress Meryall has proposed that you be allowed to reside in a remote house on the island of Bardsey, under the supervision of a cunning man, in order that you engage in scholarly endeavours to repay your debt to the people – and that you forfeit your rights and property during this period.'

Richard's eyes flicked from Carwyn to Meryall, to Lord De Lune, before he turned his eyes to the ground.

'Carwyn – please can you confirm that it is possible to put this plan in motion?'

'If you wish it, it shall be done, My Lord.'

Lord De Lune leaned back in his chair, considering the apothecary for a long moment. 'This is a dilemma indeed, Richard. The people will expect your execution. I am minded to agree with them … yet I cannot discount the justice of this plan. To end your life would be to end your suffering and to end any opportunity for reparation or rehabilitation. You are not without skills – skills which can bring income to your community. I am a man of trade, as well as the sheriff of this town. Mistress Meryall made a strong case for the worth that can be extracted from your labours. I am left with the need to understand your dangerousness and the containment that this punishment represents.'

He turned to Arledge. 'Your thoughts, sir?'

Arledge pressed his hands together before him. 'My Lord, there are few cunning folk left with the level of skill and knowledge that Richard Mangnall shows. His talents are beyond many of his generation. Gwydion ap Owain, who has resided on the Island of Bardsey for many years, is one of the few cunning folk in our realm who surpasses the apothecary in skill and knowledge. Gwydion is also skilled in the arts of protection and shielding and so would be able to limit the powers that the apothecary can exert.'

Lord De Lune rested his chin upon his clasped hands for a long minute. Meryall looked from one to the other, trying to trace a resemblance in their features. She had not told Lord De Lune that Richard was his half-brother – the court was little concerned with his motivations, but merely wanted to know the facts of the case. She did not wish to further complicate or bias the decision-making in Richard's sentencing. She rubbed her hands over her eyes. She hoped that was the right choice.

The silence in the chamber pressed in upon them all.

'The supervision of Richard Mangnall would be an onerous responsibility, Carwyn. What makes you believe that Gwydion ap Owain will be willing to do this? You cannot have had an opportunity to speak to him.'

Carwyn smiled. 'As Master Arledge indicated, Gwydion is a powerful man. We have long been friends. He gave me an amulet as a means of contacting him – using it I was able to discuss Meryall's suggestion and the history of the case with him yesterday night. He gives his consent for Richard to be sent to him, with the caveat that after five years you will review the case and consider whether he continues to require constraint.'

Carwyn turned to Richard. 'From you, he requires assurances of compliance with the conditions he imposes upon you to ensure that you are unable to harm others and that you will work hard in whatever task he requires of you.'

Richard bowed, his shackles clanking. 'I would be willing to agree to his terms.'

Lord De Lune rose to his feet, calling for the captain of his guards. 'You will be responsible for forming a party to take Richard Mangnall to the Island of Bardsey. Be ready to leave by first light.'

Meryall let in a gasp of air. The room hummed with indignation. Lord De Lune ignored Roger, gave a half bow to Meryall and walked out onto the dais to inform the crowd of the sentence.

Flushed, his breathing ragged, Richard sagged against the wall, head in his hands. Meryall touched his shoulder as she passed him. He looked up, eyes meeting hers for a moment.

Tears fell down his cheeks. He nodded to her, lips tightly compressed to stem his sobs and looked away.

She stepped out into the sunlit courtyard. A soft, benign breeze ran its fingers through her hair. Her garden would be awaiting her attention – new growth bathed in the spring warmth.

It was almost time for the new moon and time to make plans for the future. It was time to return to Horn Cottage.

About the Author

Prudence S Thomas is a Forensic Psychologist from the West Midlands, UK and a life-long book lover. This is the first novel in her fantasy mystery series. You can find out more about Prudence, keep up with her book releases and join her mailing list for sneak peaks, teasers and updates at her website: www.prudencesthomas.com

Printed in Poland
by Amazon Fulfillment
Poland Sp. z o.o., Wrocław